"Bo, we're nothing "" insisted.

"Is that right?"

"We've known each other a week."

"Yes," he replied.

"It's ridiculous to feel involved so soon."

"Right."

"You couldn't possibly have feelings for me."

"Is that me you're trying to convince, or yourself?" he asked softly.

She shook her head. "You scare me."

"I shouldn't," he chided her, and scooted his chair closer to her. He took her hand in his, drew her over to the couch. Her legs brushed his, and she flinched. At her involuntary movement, he stiffened.

Suddenly it struck her as funny, and she struggled not to giggle. "If we keep wincing every time we touch each other, we'll be jumping around like corn popping."

Slowly the tension drained from him. He pulled her hand between his. "That sounds promising."

"What?" she asked warily.

He gave her a slow, wide, unbearably appealing smile. The gold flecks in his eyes danced. "Touching each other . . . "

Suddenly, for the first time in her entire life, she *wanted* to be kissed.

WHAT ARE *LOVESWEPT* ROMANCES?

They are stories of true romance and touching emotion. We believe those two very important ingredients are constants in our highly sensual and very believable stories in the LOVE-SWEPT line. Our goal is to give you, the reader, stories of consistently high quality that may sometimes make you laugh, sometimes make you cry, but are always fresh and creative and contain many delightful surprises within their pages.

Most romance fans read an enormous number of books. Those they truly love, they keep. Others may be traded with friends and soon forgotten. We hope that each LOVESWEPT romance will be a treasure—a "keeper." We will always try to publish

LOVE STORIES YOU'LL NEVER FORGET
BY AUTHORS YOU'LL ALWAYS REMEMBER

The Editors

LEAN
ON ME

JILL SHALVIS

BANTAM BOOKS
NEW YORK · TORONTO · LONDON · SYDNEY · AUCKLAND

LEAN ON ME

A Bantam Book / November 1998

ISBN 0-553-44647-9

Published simultaneously in the United States and Canada

Bantam Books are published by Bantam Books, a division of Bantam Dou-
bleday Dell Publishing Group, Inc. Its trademark, consisting of the words
"Bantam Books" and the portrayal of a rooster, is Registered in U.S.
Patent and Trademark Office and in other countries. Marca Registrada.
Bantam Books, 1540 Broadway, New York, New York 10036.

PRINTED IN THE UNITED STATES OF AMERICA

OPM   10 9 8 7 6 5 4 3 2 1

To Susann Brailey
and Joy Abella.

I'll miss both of you
and Loveswept forever.

PROLOGUE

Clarissa Woods took a deep breath, refusing to admit her knees were shaking even though no one could see her.

She sank down to the couch, hating her weakness. As she stared at her new apartment the butterflies in her stomach mingled with awe and an unaccustomed sense of freedom.

She'd agreed to start her new job as a children's occupational therapist. She was well trained, but had worked only with adults. The following day she'd be doing what she wanted most, while living by the beach in a new city—something she'd wanted since she'd been a little girl who could still hope and dream.

An entire new life.

The implications were so fantastic, it was hard to soak it all in. Clarissa stood and crossed to the window. Even though it was closed, she could still hear the soothing pounding of the Pacific Ocean as it hit the shore. Directly below, beyond the sprawling garden in her apartment complex, was the best feature of all, the one that had finally sold her on this place.

The gated driveway.

No one could enter unless they rang her and she pressed the button to open the gate.

Clarissa smiled, her first in too long to count. She couldn't be found there, she'd been careful to leave no ties. *Very* careful.

She was finally safe from the nightmare of her past. Finally home.

ONE

"Trying to kill yourself?"

Bo Tyler grunted in response. Never a quitter, he lifted his last set of ten. Slamming the weights down, he flopped back on the bench, chest heaving, heart racing. A towel hit his face and he grabbed it.

"You're working too hard," came the gentle but admonishing voice of his receptionist/administrator and close friend. Though they were the same age, Sheila tended to fuss over him as if he were her baby brother. It usually amused him.

But not after the day he'd had. "I wish you'd remember once in a while that *I'm* the boss." He reached for another set of weights. "Not your patient."

"Hard to, when I see you doing this to yourself. You're thirty, you know, Bo Tyler, not an eighteen-year-old kid."

"Now there's a news bulletin."

"What's the matter, Bo?"

"Nothing. Go home."

"Ah. Grumpy." Sheila planted her six-foot leggy frame on a bench, which meant she planned on a lengthy lecture. Her voice softened. "Don't do this, Bo. Please, don't. You can't kill yourself over every patient. There's going to be good and bad days." Her knowing gaze ran over his unnaturally still legs. "You should know that better than anyone."

Bo let go of the weights. Deep down he knew Sheila was right. Working himself sick wouldn't help, but hell if he'd admit it to her. He sighed as he levered himself off the bench and into his waiting wheelchair.

"So, are you going to tell me what's eating at you, or am I supposed to guess?" she demanded, settling her elbows on her knees.

"It's nothing."

Persistent, she pushed, her eyes worried, her hands clasped. "It's Michael Wheeling, isn't it?"

Their latest patient. Five years old and he refused to eat and drink, much less try to keep some mobility in the only limb he had left, his right arm. "We'll get to him, one of these days."

"Of course we will." Sheila watched as he used his considerable strength to bend and pick up the barbells scattered across the floor. She knew better than to offer to help. "We've com-

pleted quite a few miracles this month alone.
Thanks to you, Bo."

He set the weights on the stand against the
wall. *"Don't."*

When did she ever listen? "What you've
done," she said, lifting a hand to encompass the
entire building. "This place you've created, it's
really special. Unique. You'll reach so many kids
who need help, kids who would've never gotten it
if you hadn't used all that money you were
awarded from your accident to build this place—"

"Stop making me sound like a hero," he said
quickly, hating when people treated him as such.
No, not a hero, he thought grimly. Not when in
the deep, dark of night he still curled into a bitter
ball over what had happened to him.

"You're no hero," Sheila agreed, sounding
amused. "You're too surly for that."

He smiled because he knew it wasn't true.
"Don't forget it."

"But if you got out once in a while—"

"I get out plenty."

"I'm not talking about the kids," Sheila said,
giving him a long look. "With people our own
age. With *women.*"

"Right."

"Stop it. You know exactly how gorgeous you
are. People look, Bo. Women look. The *old* you
would never have ignored so many come-ons."

The *old* him would have made it a personal
challenge to take on each and every one.

Things had changed. Sheila should know. People either watched him with pity, looked right through him, or refused to meet his eyes at all. And women; despite the fact he still functioned very much as a man, not too many were interested in anything past a good look. And the few that were had an air of desperation about them that usually ensured they'd be bringing up marriage by the second date.

Marriage. Bo shuddered.

Yeah, giving up women had been tough, but the alternative was tougher.

"What's wrong with marriage?" Sheila demanded, and Bo sighed as he realized he'd spoken out loud.

"Nothing. It's just not for me, that's all."

"Why not?"

"Look," he said lightly, trying not to start the argument he knew was coming. "I have enough family as it is and they bug me daily. Why would I want to get married?"

"Because it's . . ." She flashed a sheepish smile. "*Good* for you?"

Bo laughed. "My folks have been calling you, huh? Putting on the pressure?"

Her smile faltered guiltily. "Maybe."

"Don't worry. It could have been worse. They could have recruited you for the job as wife."

"Scary."

Bo retrieved the last weight, ignoring his screaming chest and arm muscles. Casually, hoping to change the subject, he asked, "Did I tell you I hired a new occupational therapist?"

"Thank you, God," Sheila said, accepting the conversation shift like the true friend she was. "When does he start?"

"*She*," Bo corrected. "Clarissa Woods. And she starts tomorrow." No one knew better than he that they were hopelessly understaffed, something he intended to fix immediately. But it was critical to him that he find exactly the right combination of staff, a group who could work together as well as apart. A family. The kids he wanted to help needed that.

Clarissa seemed perfect. She came from Texas, from a town so small, he'd had to look it up on the map. Her clinical and people skills came highly recommended. Though she'd worked only with adult accident victims in the past, her patients reportedly loved her. So did her last supervisor, who had described her as soft-spoken, but unbelievably firm. Sweet and coaxing, yet tough, resilient, and persistent.

All those things were important, of course. But they hadn't been why he'd hired her, why he'd encouraged her to come halfway across the country to California. No, he'd wanted her because the moment she'd walked in his office door for the interview and their eyes had met, he'd felt something. . . . He couldn't put his finger on it exactly, but he'd known he *had* to have her on staff.

He'd been immediately drawn to her quiet, yet surprisingly tough demeanor, her lovely, yet cool eyes, and her reluctant yet sweet smile. Both a challenge and a blessing. She would fit into his plans for his facility, *The Right Place*, perfectly. And as for how perfectly she'd fit into *his* life, well . . . he looked wryly down at himself, and his unmoving legs.

Chances were no woman would *want* to fit into his life, possibly ever. After all, the doctors had told him, with far more compassion than he'd been able to take, he would never walk again. The accident had so severely damaged the nerves and muscles in his thighs and lower legs that they couldn't function the way he needed them to for walking.

But dammit, he could *feel* them. Well, okay, not quite, but with all his heart and soul, he constantly willed them to move.

They didn't. Still, every night he worked his body ruthlessly, and knew deep down, he'd prove them all wrong. He *would* walk again. Someday. He would, or die trying.

But for now, it would be enough to spend the ridiculous amount of money he'd been awarded on children less fortunate than he. And he'd do it with Clarissa's help.

Clarissa opened The Right Place's front door, her palms damp and fisted. A blast of warm air dissipated the chill from the winter morning. The low but soothing beat of music handed her edgy spirit a boost. And the kind, welcoming smile of the receptionist gave her the courage to step in.

"Hello." The woman stood, grabbed a walker from behind her, and made her way awkwardly around her desk. "I'm Sheila. You must be Clarissa. Bo told me about you."

It was impossible not to respond to her genuine smile. Impossible, too, not to glance at the tall woman's unnaturally bent legs.

Sheila noticed. "I know, I'm an Amazon. But you should see me on the basketball court. I rule."

Basketball court? Using a walker? "I'm supposed to start work today," Clarissa said, skipping the small talk. She was horrible at it, and so nervous she couldn't manage a casual banality to save her life. "I'm a few minutes early."

Sheila's friendly demeanor reassured and calmed her at the same time. "Let me find Bo."

Nerves leaped again, making Clarissa's stomach roll. Despite what she'd hoped, her unease around men hadn't disappeared with her move across country. "Do we have to?" she blurted out.

Sheila looked startled. "He's in charge. And he's expecting you."

"I know," Clarissa said quickly, wanting to dive into the closest hole. "It's just that . . ." *Just smile, Woods.* Just shut up, smile, and work, work, work. "You don't have to bother him. You could just show me where to start."

As she spoke, the subject of their conversation wheeled into the reception area, his face creased into a warm, endearing smile. The butterflies going rampant in her stomach settled slightly. Shockingly enough, in their place came a strange sense of . . . homecoming. Since she didn't trust her feelings, she remained on guard.

"Hello," Bo said with an easy grin that should have made her feel horribly awkward, but didn't. His shoulders were wide, lean, yet roped with unmistakable sinewy strength. His arms, bent and held taut over the wheels of his chair, showed equally remarkable strength. The sight of his tanned, capable-looking limbs completely immobilized her.

But in the back of her mind it occurred to her, this man with the rich mahogany-colored hair and even richer mahogany-colored eyes, was a calm, serene man. He was also the most handsome man she'd ever met, wheelchair or not, which tensed her up all over again. Yet his eyes never strayed from her face, never once made that slow, insulting perusal of her body most others did, and she forced herself to relax.

Bo Tyler was no threat, not since she'd learned how tough she could be. No one would be a threat to her ever again.

He wheeled right up to her. "Welcome."

"Thanks." She clasped her hands tight. "Where do I start?"

Bo laughed, a nice deep sound that stirred up

the stomach flutters again. Clarissa wasn't sure it was a bad feeling, and that thought alone startled her so that she missed his next words.

At her blank expression, he simply repeated them patiently in that low, deep, husky voice of his. "Just dig right in? No preliminaries, huh?"

"Not unless you have forms for me to fill out." She stuffed her hands into her pockets as both Sheila and Bo watched her. "What's the matter?" She forced a laugh. "Did you give the job to someone else and forget to tell me?"

"Of course not," Sheila said quickly, patting Clarissa's arm. "Pay no attention to us. We're just giddy to have more help. *Give the job away*," she repeated, snickering as she turned and gestured that Clarissa follow. "Honey, with you being the only suitable person in the entire bunch of one hundred applicants, that wasn't likely."

"Me?" Clarissa squeaked, very aware of Bo following them down the hall in his chair. "You picked me out of a *hundred* applicants?"

"I'm picky."

She stopped and turned to look at Bo. "I don't get it."

"What's not to get? You're good."

She simply couldn't let it be. Her experiences were too deeply ingrained for that. "Plenty of people are 'good,' Mr. Tyler. Why me?"

"You have heart," he said simply, and wheeled past her. "And call me Bo."

All she could do was stare after him.

"Well, come on," he called over his shoulder without looking back. "As Sheila said, we're excited to have you join us. I've got lots to show you."

Dumbfounded, Clarissa didn't budge. If she hadn't been so stunned, she might have laughed. *Heart.* He thought she had heart. If he only knew, it had been destroyed years ago.

She should tell him. With a job like this, he needed to know. It would matter to him. But then she'd lose the opportunity to stay, that was certain.

Something inside her cried out in protest. This job, this wonderful, quiet little town . . . she wanted it so badly for herself. *She wanted this life.*

"Are you going to watch me ride this thing all day?" Bo asked, watching her from the length of the long hallway.

Clarissa froze for the second time in as many minutes.

Hadn't she learned never to annoy a man? Her father had been brutal, ruthless in his discipline, to the point of cruelty. She hadn't done much better with her husband, though he'd never laid a hand on her. He hadn't had to, she'd already been too cowed. No, it had taken little more than a quirk of his threatening brow to send her skittering to please him. But Dirk was dead, she reminded herself, and could no longer control her.

But her boss could.

He could, and yet . . . Bo was smiling at her, his eyes twinkling mischievously. "Didn't your mother ever teach you it's rude to stare at a man riding shotgun in a thing like this?" He gestured to his chair.

Her first instinct, to apologize profusely, was swallowed up by her second—to cover up any discomfort with sarcasm. "Didn't *your* mother ever teach you it's rude to point out a lady's failings?"

Sheila winked approvingly. "Oh, honey. I'm going to like you a lot."

"It's supposed to impress and awe you that I'm in a chair and so well-adjusted. You don't looked suitably awed."

"I don't do awe well. I also don't kiss up. I guess you might as well know that now."

"Tough, aren't you?"

"Yes." He'd be even more amused if he knew how she was shaking inside.

"Well, Ms. Tough, you're going to have to try harder to keep up the pace. Half of our kids here could race circles around you in their chairs, and they will, believe me."

"Not a chance." They had gone down a wide hallway, passing a series of patient rooms filled with bright-colored walls and toys. Ahead lay a huge gym, equally colorful and filled with equipment. Clarissa was itching to jump in. "Are you going to show me what to do or are you going to pay me to talk to you all day?"

He laughed, but Clarissa didn't. Couldn't. She'd forgotten how.

"Don't you scare her off, Bo," Sheila complained with a sudden frown.

As he looked at Clarissa she could see the kindness was still there. As was the teasing mischief. No sign of malice or a hint of sadistic intentions. "No, she won't scare off," he said quietly. "She's too curious." He tilted his head, waiting patiently for her to make the next move, clearly certain that she would.

It was a dare, a friendly one, but it was there nonetheless and Clarissa knew it.

A challenge. She rarely backed away from one, and certainly wouldn't now, no matter how much a very small, cowardly part of her wanted to. "I'm not going anywhere."

Sheila and Bo exchanged a high five, which echoed loudly down the hall.

They talked freely, laughed together. After Clarissa's last job at the medical center, where an overworked staff raced around like mad ants without a second to breathe, much less socialize, this environment would be a definite change.

Oh, yes, she was going to stay.

She was going to stay and learn to live without fear, without the constant struggle to overcome it. She was going to do it if it killed her.

And then, maybe, she'd learn to enjoy it. Enjoy life.

◆——————————◆

"Bo, darling, it's Mom. I'm so glad I caught you."

Bo rolled his eyes and glared at Sheila, who'd just paged him over the intercom for a phone call. Unperturbed, Sheila grinned broadly.

He sighed and, in his chair, turned away from her as he held the phone in the crook of his shoulder. He tried not to resent being pulled out of a basketball game with his staff, but it was hard. "Hi, Mom." And because he knew exactly what she wanted, he added, "I'm really busy."

"Some greeting!" But his mother, the local historian and town social queen, didn't seem insulted in the least. "Sheila told me you're done for the day. You just saw your last patient, and before you hang up on me for interrupting the game I know you were playing, I have two questions for you."

He rubbed his eyes. "No, I'm not married yet and yes, I washed behind my ears this morning."

"Darling!" But she laughed. "Okay, okay, so I nag a little."

"A lot." He relaxed because, though she was a pest, he loved her dearly. "Mom—"

"Bo, honey, I have someone I want you to meet. She's—"

He clenched his teeth, his tension instantly back. "I can get my own dates, Mom."

"But she's *perfect*. She's just finished her internship at General and—"

And is looking for a husband. By now he knew the routine by heart.

"Mom, why do you do this? You have seven grandchildren, why do you torture me?"

"It's my job." Her voice turned serious, as only a mother hell-bent on playing Cupid can do. "And I want you to be happy, Bo."

"I am." Why couldn't anyone believe that?

Sheila came close and let a slip of paper float down in front of his eyes. His older sister was on line two. Sheila hugged his shoulders in silent support.

"Gotta go, Mom," Bo said wearily. "Kimberly's turn to torture me now."

He punched in line two and prepared himself for a similar conversation. "Hey, Kim."

"You stood up Tess," she said, skipping the amenities. The accusatory tone she used made him feel as though he were five again, with his ten-year-old sister ruling his world. "How could you, Bo? She's a good friend."

"I didn't stand her up. We went to dinner and by the second course she wanted to know how many kids I wanted."

In his mind he was already back on the court with the guys, who could care less if he was getting laid every night. Okay, they might want to know if he was, but they certainly didn't care if he was married or not.

Kimberly, an orthodontist, wife, and mother of four, didn't understand the problem. "So?"

"So I don't want kids. I'm pretty sure I don't even want to get married."

"Bo!"

"I mean it, Kimmy." They'd had this discussion a hundred times since his accident. A *thousand*. And suddenly it made him mad. "Look at me. What kind of a dad would I be when I can't chase after a toddler? Or dammit, help train a teen for track? Or walk my daughter down the aisle?"

Silence met his tirade, but Bo continued, determined not to have this conversation again. "I'm surrounded by kids all day, kids I can give something back to. Kids I can help, Kim. It's enough for me. Let it be enough for you too."

There was a lengthy pause, and Bo realized his sister was hearing him, really hearing him, for the first time.

"Oh, Bo," she finally said, understanding in her voice. "I didn't mean to nag like Mom."

"I know. I love you, sis. Gotta go now, okay?"

"Okay. I . . . love you, too, Bo. I'm sorry."

By the time Bo got back to the court, all his staff had gone home. Let down, he wheeled through the building, shutting things off for the night.

Between Clarissa, the two physical therapists,

the speech therapist, and the three physicians, they had treated nearly one hundred patients that day. People came from two hundred miles away to this relatively new center, the one becoming known for its radical and advanced treatment.

The one that created miracles.

Bo knew it wasn't miracles at all, but hard and inventive work. By concentrating on the children's needs, by using the developmentally appropriate incentives he'd come up with, and by lavishing special attention on each child, they gave these kids a reason to try harder, to give more. It worked, amazingly well.

Yeah, they had failures, cases where absolutely nothing worked, or even worse, where through no fault of anyone but Fate, the patient died. Each time they lost someone, it got to him. So much so that he told himself he couldn't go on, he couldn't do it again. It drained too much out of him.

But then there were the successes. Teaching a three-year-old paraplegic how to live with being in a chair, or helping an eight-year-old boy use a prosthetic device. Each case was a triumph he shared. A triumph that rejuvenated him, and reminded him why he did this.

It was tough—more than tough. But Bo never gave up. It wasn't in his nature, and in fact, it was the basis for the success of this business.

As he passed the small kitchen his staff used for a break room during the day, his chair skidded to a stop.

Clarissa stood by the refrigerator, drinking from a juice bottle. Her head was tilted back, her slim, pale throat exposed as she swallowed. Her long strawberry-blonde hair, now free of its restrictive braid, flowed down her back. The white coat she'd worn all day had opened, revealing a pretty blouse tucked into fitted trousers, both of which covered a petite but gently curved frame. When she turned slightly, giving him her profile, he noted how thin she was, almost too much so.

Yet he'd seen proof today of her physical strength as she'd lifted child after child, some quite heavy, from one piece of equipment to another, never seeming to tire. She'd smiled as she worked, her firm voice encouraging, her laugh light and contagious. Fascinated, Bo could have watched her for hours, for she was a miracle unto herself. When she worked, all sarcasm and defensiveness disappeared. The tension drained from her face and body, and she sounded carefree and happy . . . yet unbelievably tough. She could coax a response from the most unresponsive child, and it had given him great joy to witness this.

She was an amazing talent.

It reflected from her to the kids she helped, and they had taken to her immediately. Bo wondered, as he had several times now, what made her tick. She had a gift, a rare one, and he didn't think she had come by it naturally. It went far deeper than merely doing her job well. Clarissa *understood* the mentally and physically challenged kids she worked with, empathized with them so completely, they felt she was one of them. Where had that understanding come from?

And where was *his* insatiable curiosity coming from? he wondered. He indulged himself by watching her another minute. There had been a time when women had been a special hobby of his. Despite his interfering family, he didn't allow himself much of that anymore because it was tough on his ego. But he could still enjoy looking.

Clarissa was beautiful and he took pleasure in the sight of her graceful movements. He must have made a sound, for suddenly she jerked, then nearly spilled her drink.

And just that fast, her innate grace disappeared, and in its place came a touching clumsiness, a self-consciousness he didn't quite understand.

"Sorry," Bo said quietly. "Didn't mean to startle you."

She avoided his gaze. "You're going to have to subpoena my guardian angel for those ten years you just shaved off my life, sneaking up on me like that."

"I wasn't sneaking. But I could put bells on my chair if you wish."

She set down her drink and shoved back a wayward strand of hair, looking annoyed instead of amused. "Just honk next time," she suggested, still not meeting his gaze.

Everyone in his life, even Sheila, treated him

like a piece of china when it came to his chair. No one ever referred to his handicap with as little reverence as Clarissa did, and though he supposed it should bother him, it didn't.

He loved it, which made him grin.

That pretty mouth of hers scowled in return.

Bo gave serious contemplation to kissing that scowl away and how it would feel. "For such a tough little thing, you shouldn't be so jumpy. What's the matter, you on the run?"

Her gaze jerked to his, and for a second a parade of emotions danced across her face. Guilt, nerves, fear . . . pain. Then, in the blink of an eye, it was all gone.

But it was too late. If there was something Bo recognized and understood well, it was fear and pain. All joking fled from his mind.

This woman he already felt attached to had been hurt, badly, he would have to tread carefully. For the first time since his accident five years before, his heart seriously warmed over a woman.

TWO

"*Are* you on the run?" Bo repeated softly.

"Maybe I just like my privacy." Clarissa's cool, blue eyes were by far the prettiest he had ever seen, and they didn't leave his face as he maneuvered into the room.

"I like my privacy too." God, she smelled wonderful, soft and feminine, and the undamaged part of his lower body responded, startling him. When had *that* last happened? "You did great today," he said a little hoarsely. "Did you like it?"

For a minute her gaze warmed. "Oh, yes." Her southern accent thickened as she forgot to curb it the way he'd noticed she typically tried to do. "The children . . . they're wonderful. Most of them are already so well adjusted."

His workout, Bo decided, could wait a minute, and he moved farther into the room that was purposely wide enough for his chair. "The day after tomorrow Michael comes in. I'm still having a problem getting him settled."

"I hope I can help."

"Anything at all will be a milestone."

She nodded, looking professional again. Not what he wanted, so he spoke before she could. "I never got a chance to ask you, how was the move? Are you all unpacked?"

"Yes."

"Going to miss Texas, I bet."

"Yeah, that muggy weather is a favorite of mine."

Her beautifully expressive face didn't fail him. Despite her light sarcasm, he'd caught the flash of melancholy before she'd masked it, and figured it was due to her recent widow status. "Miss your family?"

Carefully, she set down her drink. Without looking at him, she shed the white coat and hung it in the closet between the refrigerator and pantry. Wearing her indifference like a second skin, she said, "I'm not much for small talk."

Oh, she was something, and though he knew he was pushing, he couldn't seem to help himself. "They must have been sad to see you go."

Her eyes had shuttered at his first question, but now they turned to blue ice. "I'm sure my father is grieving as we speak. Excuse me," she murmured in a frigid voice, and moved to the door. "Good night."

Prickly *and* unwilling to discuss herself.

Which, of course, given his wild curiosity, only made matters worse. "It's a bad habit," he conceded, which stopped her.

"What is?" Her fingers rested against the doorjamb. Clearly she yearned to make a run for it.

"Delving into people's personal lives. I'm hopelessly nosy." He shrugged, but didn't apologize. How could he, when for some strange reason, he wanted to know everything about her?

"Curiosity killed the cat," she reminded him, so straight-faced, so quietly serious, he had no idea if she was joking or not.

"Well, you can see what it got me." He gestured to his still legs.

She paled. Her knuckles went white with her grip on the door. "I'm sorry. Sometimes my tongue has its own mind."

She looked so horrified, so shaken, he had to laugh. "I was kidding, Clarissa. What happened to me wasn't my fault." He left out telling her that he'd blamed himself for five long years. That sometimes, after a particularly frustrating day, when he could hardly drum up the energy to get home, he still blamed himself.

"Oh." Relief flickered over her features. Relief, and in spite of her obvious hostility, a question.

He rarely spoke about what had happened to him, but for some reason, he felt like doing so now. "I was in a car wreck. A drunk driver going seventy-five miles an hour hit me head-on."

"My God. You're lucky to be alive."

There'd been nights he'd wondered about that. "Yeah."

"What happened?"

"I was pinned beneath the steering column. My legs were crushed beneath the steel of the front of the car for two hours before they cut me free. I broke my pelvis and lower back."

Her cool exterior melted. "Oh, Bo."

"Surgery helped." He lifted a shoulder. "And I didn't have to lose the limbs, so that's something."

Her gaze told him that his cavalier attitude wasn't fooling her. God, he hated sympathy. But he'd started this, hadn't he? "Can't feel a damn thing below my thighs."

Those huge eyes of hers were moist, and with a sigh, he turned to the sink to get her a glass of water. There weren't any glasses on the counter, where he liked to keep them. "Can you reach me a glass?"

"Why?"

Craning his neck, he looked at her. "Why? Because like we just discussed, I'm in a chair. You couldn't have forgotten."

Her misty eyes blinked owlishly, but mercifully, they cleared of tears. "No. Your chair squeaks when you turn right."

Moving past him, she stretched her willowy

body over the sink. He watched, wondering if she brought her razor-sharp tongue with her when she made love, and the thought so startled him that for a minute he just gawked at her, lost in the image he'd created.

"A guy who can admit a failing," she said as she handed the glass to him, watching as he turned on the water. "Pretty impressive."

Pretty humiliating. "Here," he said gruffly, shoving the full glass at her.

She took a tiny sip. "You've come so far—"

"Don't," he said quickly, unwilling to hear the "hero" thing. "But if you still want to feel bad, you could tell me something about yourself."

"That's emotional blackmail."

"Clarissa," he said, marveling at how quickly her claws came out. "I was kidding. You're going to have to lighten up a bit, sweetheart. If not, we'll kill you with our sense of humor."

She stared at him as his words sank in. "I'm not your sweetheart."

"You're a touchy thing, aren't you?"

Her gaze narrowed dangerously. "So?"

He lifted his hands in mock surrender. "Hey, just making an observation. Last job must have been pretty rough, huh?"

"I'm just not into everyone knowing every-thing about me."

"No secrets here. If you've got a torrid past, you might as well admit it now. If not," he said teasingly, "We'll just find out by ourselves and torture you with it."

She paled at least five shades of color, if that were even possible.

Instinctively, he moved his chair forward as concern flooded him.

"Don't crowd me."

Her voice sounded weak. Concern gave way to a gut-wrenching fear. "Clarissa." He reached for her hand.

She jerked at the contact, and eyes cleared, she met his gaze. "Back off."

"Are you all right?"

Her eyes remained inscrutable. "Don't I look it?"

"No. You look like hell."

She shrugged, the casual act in complete contrast to the expression on her face. "Hey, thanks. I try."

He wasn't about to let her get away now. Not when his curiosity was eating at him. "What's the deal about your family, Clarissa?"

She clenched her purse tight to her body. "I thought this was a job, not a psychoanalytic center."

"The staff thinks of itself as family."

She fumbled back a step, groping blindly behind her for the door. "I don't need family."

"What *do* you need?"

"To be left alone."

With that, she whirled and left the room.

———◆———◆———

Clarissa fretted over her dramatic exit for most of the night as she drove home in her carefully locked car. She entered the gated condo complex she could afford thanks only to her dead husband's retirement account, and parked in her garage. Though she knew her father was still in prison, she waited until the automatic door had closed behind her before getting out. Once inside her small apartment, she shut her blinds before turning on every light in the place.

Then, when she'd changed and again checked her doors, she allowed herself to paint. Just holding her paintbrush soothed her. She loved the motions of creating fantasy, loved the feel of the wooden brush in her fingers, the scent of the wet paint, the sound of it gliding onto the canvas.

To Clarissa, painting equaled joy, and she spent long moments lost in that joy, moments when she allowed nothing else to penetrate.

She was free, truly free, and just knowing it went a long way toward easing her embarrassment over that last awkward conversation with Bo. She'd overreacted to his easy questions, and realizing it didn't help ease the heat in her cheeks.

He'd thrown her off-kilter, that was all, and it had nothing to do with his boyish good looks and easy manner. It'd been the questions about her family. So he knew her husband had died. What would he say if he knew the truth, that she thanked God for his death every night?

She'd left town without a word. No doubt her brother, Sean, a marine stationed in Germany, would worry when he eventually came back into town and found her gone, but she couldn't allow herself to think about that. Nor could she contact him, for fear her father would find her through him. She valued her new life too much.

She set her brush down, unable to be creative with her thoughts so turbulent. When, oh when, would she learn to feel at ease with herself? At ease with others, especially men? She felt comfortable enough at work, but that didn't count. Work was easy.

It was life that came so hard.

Painting was her one true love, and her one true vice. She'd been in love with the act of painting since she'd been a child, but her father never had allowed her such a frivolous hobby. He'd never allowed her any hobby at all.

Clarissa's forehead wrinkled as her concentration broke. Her hand, again poised with the brush, fell to her side. With a puff of air, she drew a deep breath and tried to erase the memories, but they assaulted her all the same.

Fast, hateful hands. Loud, harsh voices. Little food, no warmth, and constant, unwavering fear.

Bitterness was not only a waste of time, it was completely beyond her. She blamed no one but the monster who'd raised her; not the social workers, who were as terrified of him as she was, and not her own mother, who'd long before made her own escape.

But Clarissa had survived, and because she had, she could now survive anything. Including working for a man who seriously challenged her icy resolve with nothing more than his warm, kind eyes.

She'd promised herself a new beginning and she had made it. And friends. She'd promised herself friends. *Real* ones, who cared about her, about her life.

She simply had to stop jumping down people's throats when they tried to be friendly.

It would take practice, that's all.

THREE

Clarissa went into work determined to steer clear of Bo because he seemed to be the one and only person in her new life who could unsettle her.

But she was early and so was he.

She entered the kitchen to drop off her purse and jacket, then wished she hadn't. His back was to her, so she had the advantage of not being seen, and for a minute she wavered, wanting to run away. But she was hopelessly mesmerized.

Bo had a little girl on his lap, her empty wheelchair next to his.

"Coloring isn't my specialty," he was saying as he carefully directed her hand with his. Together they held a blue crayon and were drawing circles.

"I'm gooder than you." The girl giggled, and behind them, Clarissa bit her lip to keep from smiling. Cecilia was seven and had been born with Down's syndrome. Because of that, she had severe developmental problems, but already she was going to be a favorite of Clarissa's.

" 'Lissa colors with me."

"That's right. *Clarissa*," Bo said, and Clarissa wondered if she only imagined the sudden huskiness to his voice. "Do you like to color?" he asked Cecilia, their heads bent together.

"Blue."

"Blue," he repeated gently as together they drew another circle. "You're so smart, CiCi."

CiCi giggled again and kicked her legs against Bo's. His free forearm was wrapped securely around her middle as she wiggled and smiled, paying little attention to the circles, but clearly adoring the attention.

And Clarissa, who'd sworn never again to want a man's attention, suddenly found herself longing for that very thing. Bo had such a gentle, direct way about him as he talked. He wasn't pretentious or coy, he was just . . . there. A man who appreciated her.

And wasn't that just the problem? A man, an *appreciative* one, scared her to death.

At that moment Bo looked up, and caught her staring at him a bit misty-eyed. His smile was slow, warm, and she had no doubt, it was all for her.

" 'Morning," he said.

Before she could answer, Mrs. Anderson, Cici's mother, came to the doorway. "Oh, Bo, thank you. I was able to make my call in peace; a novelty."

"Good." As if Cici weighed no more than a kitten, Bo lifted her up in his arms and settled her in the waiting chair.

Before she knew it, and far before she was ready, Clarissa was alone in the room with him, her tongue hopelessly tied.

His gaze locked on hers. "Round two, or a truce?"

Where was her wit? Where was her tongue? Both had been swallowed, lost in the strange emotions he'd caused. Without a word, she turned chicken and bolted.

Bo made his way into the huge gym after a particularly rough day—one in which his newest therapist had managed to avoid speaking to him except when it pertained to a patient.

He was alone, and because he was, he worked his body ruthlessly. Then he repeated the whole regime. Sheila would have killed him if she'd found him. So would his family, or any of his staff. He overworked himself into agony, pushed his body far past its capacity.

His determination to walk haunted him.

After an hour and a half Bo slumped on the floor and struggled to catch his breath, every inch of his body on fire.

When he could draw air without wanting to

die, he strapped on the dreaded heavy metal-and-leather leg braces. It took every ounce of strength to push to a stand using a walker, his three-legged crutch.

Adrenaline surged as he stared at himself in the mirror. Standing! God, it felt good. Good, too, to see the body that had once been as finely tuned as a well-oiled machine. Still strong. Still hard. The cotton tank top he wore exposed his toned, muscled arms and shoulders, still quivering with exertion. His chest, damp from the sweat pouring off him, was broad. His belly was satisfyingly flat, rippled with muscles. But the shorts covering his lower body emphasized the atrophied thinness of his legs, made all the more prominent by the obnoxious leg braces.

He hated the way they looked, so he closed his eyes and focused on the fact that he was standing of his own accord.

Yet it wasn't enough. *Anyone* could stand.

He wanted more, a lot more.

Teetering wildly, using the walker, he pushed forward, convinced he could do it. He could walk. He *would* walk.

It took him another thirty minutes, but he made it halfway across the room.

Then, without warning, the walker slipped out in front of him and he fell flat on his face.

Swearing, trembling like a baby, he tried again.

And again, and again. But it was no use, he couldn't do it. No matter how strong he made himself, it was useless. He couldn't walk if he couldn't feel his legs.

Bruised, his ego battered beyond recognition, he lay on the mat panting and gasping. One more time, he promised himself, and painfully dragged his body upright.

He managed one last baby step with the walker, before he fell hard.

He didn't try again.

Two days later Bo watched Nathan and Jeremy, two of his patients, roll around on the mat. He had mountains of paperwork to do, a wheelchair-basketball tournament to organize, and The Right Place's annual auction to plan.

But he didn't budge, lost in the joy of watching the seven-year-olds hooting and hollering and generally having the time of their lives. So was Jeff, their physical therapist, though he seemed the only one of the three on the mat that realized the play was really work.

The large, open room was painted in bright colors and filled with toys and exercise equipment. It had been designed for workouts with kids. Now it echoed with the sounds of fun and laughter. On the other side of a wall-length mirror sat the twins' mother, Sally. Because the mirror was one-way glass, Bo couldn't see her expression, but he knew she'd be smiling at her boys' antics. Smiling and full of relief at their increasing mobility, despite their seemingly insurmountable handicaps.

At times like this everything became worthwhile for Bo. It didn't erase his own hidden pain; nothing could do that. Neither did it take away what had happened to him. He'd suffer that for the rest of his life. But somehow, it did lessen his many frustrations.

"Bend that left leg more, Nat," Jeff called out, reaching into the tangle of limbs to help direct a painfully thin leg into the right position. "Good. Jer, you got him, *you got him*. Stretch it, buddy. Go on, reach for it." He watched intently, as did Bo, as both boys worked their bodies, strengthening and gaining endurance.

Jeff continued to call out encouragement, often getting into the fray himself to show them a move. The noise level shot up a decibel when he stopped to tickle each boy, nodding his head to Bo when he found each of them limber to his satisfaction.

Giggling, Nathan and Jeremy continued to wrestle, and Bo found himself grinning at their efforts. They'd come so far. Just three years ago they'd endured the life-threatening surgery required to separate Siamese twins, and doctors hadn't expected either to live.

To be at their level was truly a milestone, and as always, the thought brought a tightening to Bo's chest. He'd helped, he thought with a flare of triumph.

It was a reminder of how much good had come out of what had happened to his own body.

"Yeah, like that, Nat," Jeff shouted, laughing when Nat held his brother down and kissed him soundly on the cheek. Jeremy growled and fought back, gaining the upper hand. "Good job, buddy, get him."

"It's amazing."

Already, Bo had committed that soft voice to memory. He looked up at Clarissa as she stood in the doorway. "Aren't they?"

A half smile tugged at her lips as she watched them. All Bo could see was her profile, her straight nose, those high cheekbones, and that soft, giving mouth that he couldn't seem to stop dreaming about. Her light hair had been hastily piled on top of her head and tendrils escaped everywhere, framing her face. She wore little to no makeup, but she had such a natural beauty to her that her fair skin seemed to glow. Her freckles, which he had already noticed with delight, were unbearably sexy. But some of his pleasure at watching her faded when he looked deeper, past the exterior to the woman beneath.

Edgy was the first word that came to mind. A lingering sense of loss. An aloneness. Again, his curiosity was piqued. She'd really stunned him the other night, with that business about her mysterious past, and though he'd love to push for answers, he knew she wouldn't allow it.

He just wished it didn't matter to him so much. It shouldn't matter. After all, he certainly had enough problems of his own. She should be nothing to him except his newest employee.

But Bo had never been able to distance himself from anything. He wouldn't start now. For some inexplicable reason, Clarissa drew him, and it'd been so long since a woman had done that, he couldn't let it go.

"I can't believe how the smaller one—Jeremy?" Clarissa looked at him questioningly until he nodded. "I can't believe how he can bend with that rod in his back. Look at him dip his neck down."

"Jeff works with them three times a week. He's performed quite a miracle."

"Sheila said the doctors told their parents he'd never walk. But just watch him!"

He wanted just to watch *her*, she so fascinated him with her intriguing mix of toughness and vulnerability. He longed to reach out and touch her, just to see if she felt as creamy and soft as she looked. "Isn't it incredible how resilient they are?" he asked, hoping she'd stay and talk this time, rather than run away.

She cocked her head and studied him.

"Haven't you noticed you're fairly resilient yourself?"

"My family would disagree with you. They see it as a personal failure that I haven't picked my life up exactly where I left it before."

"What did you do . . . before?"

In mock surprise, he let his jaw drop. "Was that—no, it couldn't have been. A *personal* question?"

She turned her back to him. "No. Forget it."

A deep flush worked up the back of her neck, making him want to press his lips to that exact spot. "So you're one of *those*," he observed, biting back both his sudden desire and laughter. "You can dish it out but you can't take it."

"I said forget it."

"I'm a basketball nut," he offered, smiling when she turned warily back. "Played it from—"

"I'm not listening," she informed him, putting her hands over her ears.

"—the time I could walk all the way through college." He knew she caught every word because her eyes watched his lips. "Then, because I couldn't get it out of my system, I coached."

She dropped her pride and her hands, shoved some hair from her face, and gave him a sheepish "I give in" look. "I've heard Sheila say at least three times that you should have gone pro."

"I should have, if you ask anyone who thinks they know what's best for me, which happens to be just about everyone I know."

"Ah." She nodded sagely. "It must be tough having people care about you."

"Sometimes it is," he answered seriously, though she'd spoken sarcastically. "I've never been able to make them understand the truth."

"Which is?"

"That I loved to play, but loved to coach even more. No one believes that, but it's the truth. At least I have an excuse now, and it keeps everyone off my back." He gestured wryly to his legs. "And my family had no choice but to forgive me for not going pro."

She looked sorry she'd asked, and he didn't want that.

"I still play. Pretty damn well, too, if I say so myself."

Clarissa's eyes smiled far before her reluctant mouth did. "So modest."

A good chunk of her armor seemed to fall away. Good humor became her, he realized. So did her smile. "Another particular talent of mine, modesty."

"I bet. I've seen your recent trophies in the office, so I'm inclined to believe you. You organize the tournaments and coach the teams. The kids thrive on that." She glanced at the twins. "I have to say, it's very encouraging to them. Gives them so much confidence, and something to hope and dream about. It works wonders."

"Yep." Bo smiled. He wondered if she noticed

how her icy facade crumbled while she was working. And he wondered if that icy facade stayed crumbled when she kissed.

Her gaze remained on the happy, wild boys, and was suspiciously bright. "I've read their chart," she said quietly. "What the boys have been through would shake the most stoic of people. You've accomplished so much . . . and looking at them—" Her lips curved as she watched them romp and play and screech. "Do they have any idea how lucky they are to have such a place as this? A city hospital certainly wouldn't give them this much care."

Everything she felt crossed her face, Bo thought. Wonder. Hope. Joy. Witnessing the gamut of those emotions, seeing what she was capable of, made *him* feel like the lucky one. "I doubt they can understand, but their family does, and that's enough."

She nodded, and as if she'd just realized how close she stood to him in the doorway, she backed up and crossed her arms over herself.

"Have I told you how happy we are that you're here?" he asked, not making a move. He sat perfectly still in his chair, willing her to loosen up.

She didn't. "You don't have to keep telling me. As long as you keep the money coming, I'm not going anywhere."

"Ah, and here I thought you wanted to work with me for the exquisite company I provide."

"*Sheila's* exquisite company." She backed another step. "You talk far too much."

He laughed. "Some people *like* to talk, Clarissa."

"Not me."

So resistant. And so apprehensive. "You didn't insult me, Clarissa. You can never insult me with the truth."

"Some people," she muttered, "don't like the truth."

"I do."

"Must make it tough," she commented. "A man like yourself. I imagine not many people are honest with you."

Her insight startled him. He fought that with her own weapon of choice. Sarcasm. "Feel sorry for me?"

She snorted. "With those looks? Fat chance."

"You know most people show *some* degree of sympathy for a man in a wheelchair."

"Why?"

He sighed. "You're difficult. Anyone ever tell you that?"

"A few."

He couldn't help himself, he had to know. "Why don't *you* feel sorry for me?"

"Because you're a man."

"Are you one of those women who hate men?"

"No, of course not." She didn't meet his gaze.

Any confidence she'd exuded before as she'd waited for her turn with her patients had fled. Anxious to give it a boost, Bo wheeled back a bit, giving her more room.

She took it and more by backing tight against the jamb.

Bo forced himself to let it go. She had made it clear she welcomed no prying about her past, though he had plenty of questions. He wanted to know if the haunting sorrow in her eyes came from missing her husband. He wanted to know if she was happy here, and planned on staying. He wanted to know how she felt about being with a man who couldn't walk.

She licked her lips and stared at him, blue eyes filled with secrets, and all of a sudden he wanted to know most of all how she felt about kissing, because despite her hands-off attitude, her lush mouth was most definitely driving him to distraction.

He'd had a dream childhood, with parents who'd spoiled him rotten with love. He'd always been easygoing, while fiercely competitive, both of which qualities won him leagues of friends. Then puberty had hit, and he'd discovered girls. They'd flocked to him, even before he'd known what to do with them. But he was a quick learner and had made the most of every opportunity that came his way.

Still, he'd never had his heart broken.

Since his accident, his incredible good luck

with women had faded. Most tended to see him as
half a man, or even worse, a quick road to a con-
venient marriage.

Being without women had been a difficult ad-
justment, but one he thought he'd made just fine.

Until now.

"You're staring at me."

He jerked back to the present, a little embarrassed at his reverie. "Am I?"

"Have I grown a third eye?" She lifted her
foot and studied the bottom of her shoe. "Maybe
I'm trailing toilet paper, or something equally
embarrassing?"

"Maybe you're just nice to look at."

"Right," she said.

"Actually, you're more than nice. You're
pretty terrific."

That certainly gave her something to think
about, given the way she chewed on her lip and
continued to stare at him.

"Hasn't anyone ever told you that before?"

"Don't," she said finally.

"Don't what?"

"Don't . . . just don't, darn it."

Unable to help himself, he grinned. "Give me
a hint. Don't what?"

"You know."

"I really don't," he said.

She rolled her eyes. "Fine." She looked
around her quickly, then apparently satisfied no

one was paying them any mind, she said, "I don't want you to flirt with me."

"Why? It's fun."

"It makes me uncomfortable," she said.

"Because I'm in a chair?"

FOUR

Clarissa gaped at him.

"Is it because of the chair?" Bo asked again, his voice a gruff whisper.

"That's a stupid thing to say," his defensive, beautiful employee informed him crossly, frowning.

"I don't think it is."

Clarissa sighed heavily, then dropped her gaze to her feet. "You being in a chair has nothing to do with this, Bo. I shouldn't have been snapping at you like that. Please believe me."

She lifted her head. Her eyes were clear, and so deep he could have drowned. "It's me," she said. "*Really*. I just . . . want to work here. That's all. No complications."

"No complications," he repeated, trying to understand. "And joking around with me is a complication?"

"Letting you flirt with me is."

Two members of his staff, Conner and Raylene, passed them in the hall. Conner, the speech therapist, slapped Bo on the shoulder in a congratulatory way. "Hey, Bo. I made progress today with Timmy. You should see the kid say 'lion' now!"

Timmy, a four-year-old born with severe palate deformities, had been through a series of operations to give him a tongue. He had barely mastered talking, and it was nearly impossible to understand him. "Good job."

He grinned up at Clarissa as they left. "Another milestone today."

Her own triumphant smile faltered. "Sheila told me you sponsor Timmy here for free because his parents can't afford the care and the state can't help. You give him full treatment. Even though you don't get a penny out of it."

Hell, that hero thing again. "You could make a lot more money being a therapist in a county-sponsored hospital, don't you think?" he asked.

She lifted a shoulder and sniffed indifferently. "Maybe I have a good reason for working here."

"Me?" Hope gleamed in his eyes while he gave her a crooked smile.

She studied him over the tip of her nose. "You don't have much of a confidence problem, do you?"

"I'm beginning to, around you."

She refused to let him deter her from business.

"I worked with Timmy earlier, you know. He's getting better with a spoon. Twice he managed to scoop off the food by himself and get it to the back of his throat."

"Yes, I know. Why won't you talk about yourself?"

"Because. Are you going to fire me now?"

"*Fire* you?" he asked incredulously. "Whatever for?"

"Because I'm not going to let you flirt with me."

He nearly laughed, until he saw how serious she was. Her shoulders were stiff, her hands fisted. By making her uncomfortable he was hurting her, and that distressed him, because he knew better. "I have no intentions of letting you go, Clarissa."

"Hmmph."

"Such faith." What the hell kind of supervisor did she have before? he wondered. Why was she so on edge? It wasn't good for her, it wouldn't be good for anyone. "You know, letting people get to know you isn't exactly painful. Just ask my mother, or any of my siblings. They call daily to find out if I've let my future wife get to know me yet."

Her eyes bugged and the arms she'd crossed defensively across her chest dropped. "Your *wife?*"

Ah, an honest reaction at last. "Luckily I haven't met her yet."

"I think . . ." Clarissa paused, studying him

as if he were an alien. "You're all a little crazy here."

"For each other."

Her look told him she was convinced her own opinion had been the correct one.

"We're a family," he clarified.

"Family." Clarissa knew she said the word as if it were a foreign expression, and she struggled to lighten up. "Is that why Sheila dumped a full cup of ice down Jeff's back earlier?"

Bo grinned roguishly, looking young and boyish, and far too handsome for his own good. It was so easy to forget he was in a wheelchair. He seemed so healthy, so vibrant. So alive. His eyes sparkled and his voice sounded carefree, husky enough to make her take a good step backward because something bizarre occurred to her.

She found him attractive.

Good Lord. How had *that* happened? He leaned close to speak to her and his shoulders bunched, leaving her with the most absurd urge to spread her hands over them. She took another step back and crashed into the wall.

"Careful," he said absently, as if having a hopelessly klutzy therapist was an everyday occurrence. "I wouldn't worry about Jeff and the ice. He'll get Sheila back. It's all in fun, you know. Sheila will *expect* him to retaliate."

"She'll . . . welcome it?"

He laughed. "She'll be disappointed if he doesn't." His amusement died at her obviously concerned expression. "No one will get hurt, Clarissa. It's just fun."

"Fun. Yeah, I can see why getting ice thrown down my clothes would be fun."

"It's all harmless."

While chaos continued to reign in the room in front of them, Clarissa searched Bo's face for a long moment. She didn't know how to put words to the feelings that coursed through her every time she was around him. He made her nervous, yet giddy. Happy, yet frightened. She felt like a sixteen-year-old with her first crush, only she'd never been anything as innocent as a teenager struck by puppy love. "*I* take you very seriously."

Bo drew a deep breath. "That's interesting," he said with an underlying sensuality that captivated her. "Because I take you very seriously as well, but I'm not sure why. We don't know each other at all, and yet I feel like I've known you for years."

She swallowed hard but refused to retreat. "I bet you say that to all your staff."

Ruefully, he fingered his chair, waiting until a nurse passed them in the hall before admitting, "I'm not exactly a success with women these days."

She ran her gaze over his legs. His injury started at his thighs, which meant all the other more critical parts were in working order. The knowledge made her tingle with awareness. She met his suddenly hot gaze. Answering heat flooded her cheeks. She'd been caught staring!

"Before this conversation goes any further, you should know I'm not interested in sleeping with anyone, physically challenged or not."

Bo knew that. And he would be a fool to harbor hopes and dreams about her. An absolute fool.

Ah, hell. Every man had his faults. "I'm not asking you for anything you're not willing to give."

She looked at him solemnly, as if weighing his every word. "And I'm not willing to do anything that doesn't directly involve the benefit of The Right Place."

He told himself it had nothing to do with his legs. That she was clearly a woman who'd had it rough in some way and was just extraordinarily cautious.

"If this is going to be a problem . . ." She crossed her arms and looked prim and uptight. "Say so now and I'm outta here."

"Oh, would you stop that?" He lowered his voice, glancing at the twins and Jeff, still happy in their play. "It's at least the third time you've threatened to go, and one of these days you're going to feel you have to follow through on your word. Then I'll have to beg you to stay, and you'll think I'm flirting with you when all I'm trying to do is save you your job and me a lot of paperwork."

"I never know what to say to you," she said, visibly relaxing.

"You could just throw ice down my shirt, like Sheila would."

"Not my style."

The bantering stirred him. So did the inexplicable tug of desire he felt for her. He'd never before met a woman he wanted to laugh with and make love to at the same time. "You could try just talking to me," he suggested hopefully. "Telling me about yourself, your past."

"Why would you want that?"

"So I could understand what or who hurt you so badly that you can't relax and enjoy anything unless you're working."

"Stop getting into my head!"

Bo took a huge chance, and rolled a little closer. She didn't try to escape, as he'd expected, and he decided that was a great first step. "I don't know what's going on in that sharp, pretty head of yours, Clarissa. But you're safe here. Your job is safe."

She didn't move, didn't speak, just turned her head and watched the action going on in the gym.

"I like my job," she said quietly.

"Because of the kids?"

"Partly." She stared at the twins still playing with Jeff, who in turn was making the most of their time together, strengthening and encouraging mobility. "But it's also the staff."

He wondered if she was including *him* in that

group. He hoped so. "I'm glad." He reached out and touched her hand. She flinched, but he ignored it, moving slow and steady. He squeezed her fingers gently with his, his heart squeezing along with their hands at the look of bewildered pleasure on her face. "I like you, Clarissa."

That clearly flustered her. Finally, apparently satisfied he meant nothing deeper, that his words had no hidden meaning, she dipped her head in acceptance. "If you'll excuse me, I have patients to see."

But she stared at their joined hands for a long moment before breaking the connection and walking away.

By the end of the day Clarissa had done one of the things Bo had asked of her. She'd relaxed. She'd worked hard, incredibly so, seeing fourteen patients; all of whom required lifting, moving, turning, shifting, coaxing. Every muscle ached and throbbed.

But so did her jaw—from smiling.

Incredible as it seemed, she was having the time of her life.

She also, for the first time in . . . well, forever, felt safe. Whole. Happy.

It amazed her, this sudden and complete happiness. She felt so light, she could have flown through her duties. And if a small part of her was aware that her newfound joy was due in part to

Bo's strength and kindness, she chose not to think about it.

After all, lifelong habits died hard, and while a good portion of her reservations and fear had vanished, some part of her would always be skittish when it came to a man.

In the kitchen, she downed an iced tea, then stiffened automatically when she heard someone enter the room behind her. Seeing Sheila, she let the tension drain immediately.

"Great day," Sheila said, letting go of her walker to plop her gangly frame into a chair. "Ah . . . sitting feels so damn good." She sighed gustily and used her hands to spread her long, thin legs out in front of her. "Don't ask me why I torture myself with that thing." She jutted her chin out, gesturing to her walker.

"Do you have a choice?" Clarissa asked.

"Sure. I could use a chair, like Bo. I'd gain speed and some semblance of grace." She laughed, shook her head. "But there's just something so freeing about using my legs, tired as they make me." She looked at Clarissa. "It's so good to have you here, you know. You really lighten the load."

They'd seen so many people today, it'd been chaotic, frantic, and immensely satisfying. "I don't know how much I really helped."

"A lot, trust me. And it's sure nice to have another woman around. Someone to help me when I get ganged up on."

"Seems to me, you only got ganged up on when *you* started it," Clarissa said, smiling.

"They asked for it, believe me."

Clarissa lifted her drink to her lips. "Did they?"

"Well, maybe not. But in Jeff's case, I can't think of any other way to get myself invited into his pants."

Clarissa nearly choked on her drink, certain she hadn't heard correctly, until Sheila laughed.

"I've shocked you," she said.

Clarissa mopped up the tea she'd just spilled at the image Sheila had put into her head and tried to be nonchalant.

It was impossible.

She sank to the closest chair and reminded herself that normal women craved sexual relations. Ironic, she thought, *she* seemed to be the handicapped one around here.

"And after I get into those gorgeous jeans he wears so well," Sheila went on, "all I have to do is convince him to be the father of my children."

Now Clarissa did choke, cursing herself for daring another sip. It simply wasn't safe to drink around Sheila.

"What's wrong, you don't want kids?" Sheila asked, her question deceptively innocent.

Much to Dirk's fury, Clarissa had never gotten pregnant. Her doctor had insisted, after a series of torturous tests, that there was nothing physically wrong with her. But since Dirk had refused to be tested, she could never be sure. "I don't know," she said.

"You'll get into it," Sheila said with certainty. "Believe me. Most of the staff are men, and they're all pretty irresistible."

"I think I can hold myself back." Clarissa firmly set her drink away from herself.

"But why would you want to?" Sheila stretched, then lifted an eyebrow suggestively. "We've got it all here, you know. Great job. Great pay. Great kids to work with. And fabulous, fit, hunky, educated guys. It's heaven."

An unbidden image of Bo settled in Clarissa's mind, startling her. She didn't dream about men; she didn't even like to *think* about them. But somehow Bo was different. He'd gotten past the first of her many barriers and she didn't know how she felt about that. Uneasy, she rose to the sink to wash out her glass.

"Take Bo, for example."

Clarissa splashed water down the front of herself.

Sheila ignored this. "He's my best friend, you know."

Clarissa thought of Bo's warm, probing eyes, which saw so much more than she wanted. She pictured his hands, large and gentle, as they helped a child in therapy, always pushing and coaxing, always easy. Never rough.

She knew damn well Bo didn't seem threatening because he was in a wheelchair, because he couldn't stand upright and be tall and menacing, but that knowledge so shamed her, she couldn't speak for a moment. "I didn't know."

Sheila watched her carefully. "He's been to hell and back. First with the accident, then getting this place going. He's been tense lately, especially with his family bugging him about starting a family."

"Sounds like they care very much."

"Yeah, they do. I keep telling him he could skip the commitment part of the whole thing and just use a good—" Sheila cut herself off at Clarissa's alarmed expression, and stretched her lips over her teeth while she searched for the right word. "Diversion," she finished diplomatically.

"I'm not into . . . *diversions* myself," Clarissa said weakly, just the thought making her a little queasy.

Sheila nodded as if she understood perfectly. "You're shy. That's all right too. Don't stress over it."

"How do you know I'm shy?"

Sheila's smile was like a warm balm over her chilled soul. "Because when you're upset or nervous, your accent comes out quite thick." She laughed at Clarissa's blush. "But I like it. It's so ladylike. So's your figure." She sighed as she glanced down at her mile-long legs. "I'd love to be small and dainty. Ladylike. Then Jeff might . . . Ah, well. Never mind. Let's talk about you. And Bo."

"I hardly know him." What had he said? *We don't know each other at all and yet I feel like I've known you for years.* She felt the same, but would have denied it if asked.

"Sure you know him. What you see is what you get with Bo." Sheila looked at her like a sly wolf making a deal with Little Red Riding Hood. "Tell me what you see."

"Well . . ." Clarissa felt silly at her reluctance. How hard could this be? "He's cocky."

"Every man is. What else?"

"He's sharp as a tack and likes to laugh."

"Too easy."

"He's . . ." She thought of how wonderful he was with the children. How easily he opened them up, how much he cared. "Compassionate." The way he looked at her sometimes, as if he could read her mind, see right past her barriers and feel her pain, that told her a lot about him as well. And though she could hardly believe she was saying it, she added, "Intuitive. Strong-willed."

Sheila roared with laughter, nearly falling off her chair. "Nosy as a child and stubborn as a jackass, you mean."

"Well . . . Yeah." She thought he was probably optimistic, especially given his circumstances, and an incredible romantic, which, instead of terrifying her as it should have, gave her a secret thrill.

"Oh, I almost forgot." Sheila straightened and

slapped her forehead. "Someone called for you a while ago, but I couldn't get a message, sorry."

The tension seized Clarissa again as every muscle in her body went on full alert. Carefully she put down the towel she'd used to dry herself. She'd given no one the number to call her. "What?"

"Yeah, someone called for you. Of course it was during a time where I had four other lines going, one of which involved an irate parent who was demanding to know why we hadn't been able to make her daughter see again. I mean, we can work miracles, but come on. Even The Right Place has its limits." She smiled, but it faltered at Clarissa's shocked expression. "What's the matter, honey?"

"Who was it?"

Sheila waved her hand. "Oh, you don't know this patient yet."

"No." Clarissa dragged a deep breath past lungs refusing to function. "I mean who called for me?"

"Oh, that. Like I said, I don't know. They didn't want to leave a message."

No one, absolutely no one, knew where she was. Just that fast, her brand-new confidence shattered. "Why not, do you think?"

Sheila shook her head, lifted a bony shoulder. "Wouldn't say. Just said he'd try again another time."

He. Oh, God. A *he*.

"Clarissa?"

She could hear Sheila's concerned voice, and struggled to shoot her a reassuring smile. But it was difficult, given the way her pulse raced. Sweat pooled at the base of her spine.

"Honey?"

He's dead, she reminded herself. *Dirk is dead.* But her father wasn't.

FIVE

In the fog of terror that surrounded her, Clarissa became aware of a familiar squeak. She knew that noise, knew it to be the sound the right wheel of Bo's chair made when he turned in that direction.

Blinking, she saw Bo's gaze on her, his face tight with worry. "What's the matter?" He reached for her with his big hands.

She leaped up, wrapped her arms around her middle in a gesture she recognized as pure defense, and backed up. "Nothing. Nothing at all."

"Honey—" Sheila started, only to stop when Clarissa shook her head sharply.

"I'm fine. Really," she added at their doubtful stare. "I just had a bad moment, that's all."

"Because some guy called for you?" Sheila stood also, reached for her walker, and pushed past Bo. "Honey, are you in some kind of trouble?"

"No, of course not." She grabbed her purse and moved toward the door. "Just tired, that's all. I'll see you tomorrow."

Bo knew she was lying. A quick glance at Sheila told him she thought the same thing.

"Something's wrong," Sheila announced when Clarissa had left. "I can feel it, Bo. She's hurting inside."

The part of him that wanted to heal everyone's hurts ached to help. The part of him that was falling for the quiet beauty yearned to ease her pain. "I know. But she won't let me get too close. I think I scare her."

Sheila snorted. "You? Get real. You're a pussycat without claws. A lion without the roar. A bee without the stinger—"

"I get the picture," he said with exasperation. "And I'm not *that* tame, thank you very much. Who called for her?"

"A man. He wouldn't leave his name and I didn't think anything of it—until I saw the terror on Clarissa's face. She seemed to know who it was."

That's what Bo was afraid of. Without another word, he wheeled to the door.

"Bo?"

He paused impatiently, his hand on the knob.

"Tell her how much we care."

"I will," he promised, though he knew that would be easier said than done. The Clarissa he was beginning to know seemed out of her element when it came to personal relationships. She wouldn't be comfortable when he spoke of such things.

Too bad, he thought, racing down the hallway at top speed, his arms pumping with the effort. He'd never been good at bottling up his feelings, as he suspected Clarissa was. He wasn't the type to shove hurt inside and pretend it didn't exist, and he had no intentions of starting now.

Clarissa pulled out of the parking lot just as Bo came to a screeching halt. Chest heaving from his effort, he sat there in the middle of the lot, watching her go.

Bo had always been intuitive, but after his accident he'd become even more so. In the pit of his stomach he had a tight, ugly feeling that wouldn't let up.

Without stopping to debate the wisdom of the move, he wheeled to his Bronco. He lost precious time disassembling his chair. But within two minutes he'd stuffed the four different chair parts behind the driver's seat and hauled himself up behind the wheel.

He snapped open his cell phone while he started the engine and dialed Sheila, who was still inside the office. In order to work the handle controls of his specially equipped car, he tucked the phone into the crook of his shoulder. "I need her address," he said the instant Sheila picked up.

She had it ready, and repeated it twice as Bo committed it to memory.

"You're going after her."

"Yeah."

He could feel her smile over the line. "Good. She needs you, Bo."

"What's this?" he teased as he pulled out of the lot and headed toward the highway. Clarissa was nowhere in sight. "Is this the same woman who for the past five years has been constantly worried about *my* needs?"

"You're fun to fuss over," she admitted. "But the truth is, you're pretty self-sufficient."

"Now's a fine time to tell me," he pointed out, whipping around a much slower truck. The Pacific Ocean pounded the shore to his left as he headed north.

"I like her."

"I like her too." The image of Clarissa's haunted face came to him and he sped up a little.

"She pretends to be so tough, so sure of herself, but I think she's really frightened of something."

"She'll be all right, Sheila."

A few minutes later Bo wasn't so sure. He sat in his Bronco outside the gated entry to Clarissa's condo.

She didn't answer his ring on the intercom.

He waited a minute more, then tried again.

Finally, she answered, her voice low and rough.

"Clarissa." Relief filled him. She'd made it home all right. "It's Bo."

Silence.

"Clarissa?"

"Why are you here?" She asked.

"Can I come up?"

"No. *No.*"

Demands would get him nowhere. Neither would a calm request. He knew her well enough to know exactly how to get to her. "You've got to give a poor lame guy a break here, Clarissa. I chased you so fast, I'm about to bust a lung."

"You're in better shape than anyone I know. Try again."

"Okay, how about I need my ego stomped on?"

"No go."

He heard the fine tremor in her voice and he wanted like hell to have five minutes with whoever had hurt her. Whoever was still trying to hurt her. "Please," he said quietly, allowing his own need to come through in his voice. "Please let me in."

He held his breath and waited.

Clarissa held her breath too. In her condo, still holding the paintbrush she'd just grabbed, she sat down and set her forehead to her knees, holding the receiver to her ear. "Why?" she whispered, squeezing her eyes tight.

"Just to talk, Clarissa," Bo said in a very unthreatening tone. A calm voice. A voice with need in it, need for her.

She had no idea why that didn't scare her to death, but it didn't.

Still . . . all she knew about him was that he paid good and cared about others. Okay, she knew more than that. She knew he was the first man in her life that had made her notice the details. Like his rich, deep, passionate eyes. His thick, wavy hair that her fingers itched to touch. He was the first man with whom she'd ever let her guard down enough to be able to look at him objectively. He was also the first man she'd considered . . . attractive.

She could look at him this way because he couldn't walk, and it was so wrong to think this that heat flooded her face. She squeezed her eyes tighter.

She set her icy hand to her cheek to cool it, thankful Bo couldn't see her. She'd driven home with the shakes, but just opening her paints had calmed her somewhat.

Her father couldn't possibly have found her. She had to believe that. Besides, even if he did, she would never again be a victim. Never.

"Okay," she said, lifting her head to stare at her easel, the one that held her latest unfinished seascape. "For one minute."

"One minute," he vowed, and clicked off.

The next few minutes were torture as she

waited, chewing her nails, while Bo parked, put his chair back together, and rolled up her walk.

He waited quietly while she unbolted, unchained, and unlocked her door. She stared down at him, watching his generous, unsmiling mouth, his sober, sharp gaze as it ran quickly over her.

"You okay?" His hands were poised over his wheels, his upper body tense as he waited for her answer.

What was it about him that made her knees weak? She'd never experienced that before. "I'm fine. What did you want to talk about?"

A corner of his mouth quirked. "Do you think I can come in?"

"Ah, okay." She realized she still held her paintbrush. Old reflexes had her hiding it behind her back with a furtive movement that annoyed her. This was Bo, not her father or Dirk, both of whom would have been furious to find her painting. But Bo couldn't control what she did with her time. She moved backward, allowing him room to wheel into the room.

He glided past her, his neck craning as he looked around him. She knew what he was seeing. The high vaulted ceilings that kept the small but cozy living room from seeming claustrophobic. She hadn't brought any furniture with her, hadn't wanted any reminders of her previous life. And since she'd spent all the money Dirk had inadvertently left her on the actual condo, and since she hadn't yet received a paycheck, she'd purchased only a couch. And painting supplies. She loved this place with a passion, and when she looked at this room she saw its potential.

Still, she was painfully aware of how bare and spartan it looked now, just as she was aware of how exposed she felt with her partially complete painting behind the couch, in front of the huge picture window.

She wished she'd covered it.

Bo only smiled. "This is nice, Clarissa." His chair squeaked as he turned and wheeled straight to the window, and her painting. "The view is spectacular."

He studied the picture she'd been working on. "Your painting is spectacular too. I had no idea you were so talented."

"I'm not. It's just a hobby," she said. She stood in front of it and took a deep breath and held it, some inner part of her needing to protect that painting.

As usual, she got nothing by Bo. He tilted his head. "Why do you do that?"

"Do what?"

"Diminish your talents like that. You're the best therapist I've got, yet you honestly don't believe it." He lifted a hand toward her easel. "This painting should be on the wall of some gallery. In fact, a father of one of our patients owns one, I can introduce you—and I can tell by how many shades of color you just lost what you think of that idea."

Clarissa had wanted to be an artist for as long as she could remember. Once, an interested, kind teacher had given her a set of supplies. Clarissa had been eight. She'd painted her heart out, using an entire pad of paper.

Her father had been furious at the waste, and in the blink of an eye had destroyed every last picture. He had thrown away the paints and forbidden her ever to lift a brush again.

Then he'd beaten her so she wouldn't forget. She hadn't.

Until she had gotten married. One of the early congratulation gifts she'd received had been from an old acquaintance. She had sent a set of paints.

Dirk had been even less thrilled than her father, and while he hadn't physically hurt her, he'd subjected her to one of his silent rages, which had effectively destroyed her creativity.

Now, with her father far away and Dirk dead, she had just gotten used to her new freedom, to knowing she could actually go to a store and buy paints, then open them whenever the mood struck her. But it still felt so fresh, and she was so unsure of herself. To think of actually approaching a gallery made her want to throw up.

She could hardly explain this to Bo.

Defensive, she crossed her arms. "Why are you here?"

Those dark, fathomless eyes hit hers. "I wanted to make sure you were all right."

"I told you I was." God. Those eyes. They

made her see things, feel things, hope for things she had no business thinking about. "Your minute is up." She moved past him, intending on going to the front door and opening it in invitation for him to leave.

His hand snaked out, surprisingly fast, and grabbed her wrist, halting her.

She tugged, but his grip, though gentle, was unbelievably firm.

So was his mouth, his tone. "Look, before we go any further with this, there's something I've got to know. Do you shut me out because of this?" He waved his free hand over his still legs.

She was silent for a minute, shocked that he could even think that. Even more shocking was the realization that if she were to let any man into her life ever again, it would be Bo, and it would be *because* of his chair.

How he would hate that, knowing she let him this close to her because of his inability to walk. "I shouldn't have to tell you anything. We're nothing to each other."

"Is that right?"

"We've known each other a week."

"Yes."

"It's ridiculous to feel involved so soon."

"Right."

"You couldn't possibly have feelings for me."

He slanted her an indecipherable glance. "Is that me you're trying to convince? Or yourself?"

Heat flooded her face. "Okay. I don't *want* us to be anything to each other."

Now those dark eyes warmed as his manner softened. "It's too late for that and you know it."

"But we've only known each other for days! I've known people my entire life who never get as close to me as you have in just that time," she cried. "You scare me."

"I shouldn't," he chided gently.

"Well, you do."

He grimaced, then shoved his hands through his hair. The movement brought Clarissa's attention to his upper arms, to the muscles bulging against the sleeves of his T-shirt.

This was a man who worked with children. Who laughed with their triumphs and cried with their defeats. He would never hurt her, she reminded herself. Never.

Still, her mouth went dry at the show of strength.

Slowly, he scooted his chair closer. Much more lightly this time he took her hand. Without a word, he wheeled to the couch, then gently pushed her into it. Her legs brushed his.

The contact startled her, made her flinch back.

At her involuntary movement, he stiffened.

Knowing he probably thought he disgusted her, which was amazingly far from the truth, she covered her face with her hands in mortification. But suddenly it struck her as funny and she struggled not to let out an inane giggle. "If we keep wincing every time we touch each other," she whispered between her fingers, "we'll be jumping around like corn popping."

Slowly the tension drained from him. Just as slowly he reached forward and pulled her hands from her face. He kept one of them sandwiched between his, lightly running his thumb over her knuckles. "That sounds promising."

"What?" she asked warily. "The corn popping?"

"No. Touching each other."

"You're—you're crowding me again."

"Am I?" he murmured, looking innocent. "I like it."

"I don't." But her eyes, as if of their own accord, stared at his mouth, her own opening slightly as thoughts raced through her head. Thoughts totally and completely foreign came to her, such as how those lips might feel against hers.

He laughed softly, the sound too sexy for her own comfort. His thumb stroked her lower lip, his eyes following the movement with a hunger that unnerved her all the more. "I love your voice." His tone hushed. "It's really beautiful." Again he stroked her lip, and she had the most ridiculous urge to suck his finger into her mouth.

He reached up and brushed a strand of hair back, tucked it over her ear, his movements gentle. Tender. She'd never been this close to him before. She could see every line on his face. His brown eyes were dusted with gold flecks. His hair, messy from when he'd shoved his hands through it, fell to the top of his collar in waves. He shot her a crooked smile that did something to her chest, made it tighten in a way that wasn't completely uncomfortable.

Suddenly, for the first time in her entire life, she *wanted* to be kissed.

As if he could read her mind, Bo leaned forward and set his lips to hers in a connection as giving and passionate as his gaze had been only a moment before.

SIX

Clarissa had never been set on fire by a kiss. She burst into flame, as if she were a dry and restless prairie dying from a season of no rain. Bo stroked her mouth with his, and she gripped his forearms and held tight. When he coaxed her mouth open with his teasing tongue, she tentatively met it with her own. A low growl of passion sounded from his throat, and she melted on the spot.

The kiss was fierce but tender. Clarissa felt the barely leashed restraint in his arms and knew, if she made the slightest protest, he'd let her go. His amazing control only fueled her sudden, ravenous hunger, and instinctively, she threw her arms around his neck and hugged hard.

She had grown up fantasizing about a gentle man, someone opposite the father who had given her only negative, abusive attention. When she'd gotten married, she held on to the fantasy, but it hadn't been meant to be.

Dirk hadn't been physically abusive, but he hadn't been physically anything. From the day she'd married him, he touched her when absolutely necessary—they'd had sex to relieve his frustration, but it had done nothing for hers. Not once had she felt even a tremor of a response. As a result, she'd long before buried any healthy sexual feelings she might have had.

Or so she had thought.

The gentleness of Bo's hands and the fire of his mouth plagued her senses, leaving her hot, needy, confused, and desperate for more. Memories and insecurities took a backseat as she lost herself in their unbelievably delicious kiss. The brush of a day's growth of beard, the scent of clean, warm male skin, the chill of the late-afternoon air combined with the warmth of Bo's arms—it all consumed her.

Threading his fingers through her loose hair, Bo held her face with his hands when at last he lifted his head. His breathing was rough, ragged, and his expression told her she hadn't been the only one to get unbearably excited.

"I've been this far with a woman," he said, holding her gaze, "since my accident."

Clarissa imagined him holding and touching a faceless woman, and found it difficult to breathe.

"But I've been no further." His mouth went

grim. "Each time it wasn't me to pull back, but . . ."

When he trailed off and closed his eyes, dropping his forehead to hers, Clarissa understood. A flash of anger filled her. Why were people so cruel? From somewhere within came a strength she hadn't realized she possessed, and she reached out to him, smoothing her hands over his shoulders. At the tough sinew beneath his shirt, she wanted desperately to yank her fingers back, but she didn't. Instead, she swallowed hard and spoke. "Whoever you were with didn't want to go through . . . with the rest of it? Because of your legs?"

He jerked his head in a sharp nod, and she ached for him.

But then the implications of what they'd done set in, and if Clarissa thought she couldn't breathe before, she'd never been so wrong.

He expected her to pull back as well, and of course she would. "Bo . . ."

Her soft tone spoke for itself, and he immediately pulled back. "I understand." Without another word, he set his hands on the wheels of his chair and whirled himself around.

Clarissa stared at his stiff, proud shoulders, at the straight, unbending line of his spine, and wanted to cry.

All her life she'd been passive. Now, when she was strong enough, free enough, to finally make decisions for herself, she was being asked to make one that would affect another.

She wasn't *that* strong!

She couldn't let him leave with things as they were either but she didn't have the foggiest idea how to fix this. "Bo, would you like some tea?"

He craned his neck around and stared at her. "Tea?"

She bit her lip and nodded.

"Tea," he repeated with a short laugh. Her hair, mussed from his hands, fell about her shoulders when she nodded again. Nervousness filled her eyes, effectively draining his frustration. She was offering him a truce, he realized. "Tea would be nice." He'd rather have something much stronger, something that would take away the unbridled heat she'd created between his thighs.

Still chewing on her lip, eyes a bit wide and wild, she spun around and practically ran into her kitchen.

He wheeled himself over to the huge window and took a deep, cleansing breath. "Tea," he muttered before he swore softly.

A phone rang, startling him out of his thoughts. An answering machine on the floor by the couch picked up after one ring. Clarissa's message was short and to the point. At the accompanying beep, he heard a man's voice.

"Clarissa, it's me, Sean." A loud sigh echoed in the room. "God, sis, I've gone through hell to find you. Call me back. I *have* to talk to you, *have* to see you."

The machine clicked off.

Bo stared at it. *Sis?*

When he lifted his head, Clarissa stood in the doorway to the kitchen, staring at the machine as if it might reach up and bite her.

Bo frowned. In the wake of the most explosive kiss he'd ever had, he'd nearly forgotten, but something was wrong, very wrong.

He came from a big family. Despite their interference in his life, he'd always felt wanted, had always been made to feel special. He knew it was due to his support system and its built-in unconditional love that he had managed to survive his accident.

It was difficult to imagine why Clarissa looked shell-shocked just at hearing her brother's voice.

He moved toward her, not surprised when she suddenly propelled herself into action, pacing the room away from him.

"I need to . . ." She paused, looked around her. "Walk," she finished. "I need fresh air."

He followed her to the door. When their fingers brushed together over the handle, she again stared at him, as if surprised to see him. "When I let you in, you said you needed just a minute," she whispered, her eyes huge in her pale face. "It was up a long time ago."

"Can I have another?"

"To *talk*, you said." She swallowed, licking her lips. "We didn't do much talking."

"No." Reaching for her hand, he squeezed reassuringly. His other hand settled at her waist. Beneath his fingers, her stomach muscles tightened. So wary, so vulnerable. His heart clenched because he suspected it wasn't anticipation that made her so nervous, but just his presence. "We didn't do much talking before," he said softly. "But I'd like to now."

"I can't."

She was wound so tight, he knew she'd explode if she didn't relax. Kissing her again wouldn't help, so he said, "Let me walk with you."

With a frankness that would have made him laugh in any other situation, she looked pointedly down at his chair, at his unmoving legs.

"I think I can keep up with you," he said dryly.

Behind them, the phone rang again. Clarissa stiffened, then quickly yanked the door open, letting the chilly early-evening air in. "Fine, come with me then." She slammed the door the minute his chair cleared the jamb.

She wrapped her arms around her middle and paused, staring at the door in abject misery.

Bo took her hand and tugged, but he had to let go of her to steer his way down the path. Dark had fallen early, but the way was well lit. They walked through the lovely gardens, bathed in the scent of year-round California wildflowers. As they went they were serenaded by the surf hitting the shore on the other side of the wall.

After a few minutes of silence, Clarissa spoke. "You're wondering."

He passed a towering palm tree and came to a bench. To the right was the ocean, which he could see through the tall fencing. He listened for a minute, enjoying the sound of the tide, before he answered her. "I'm wondering a lot of things, yes."

She studied him. "Why aren't you asking about them?"

She expected him to grill her, which was exactly why he wouldn't. He patted the bench. "Sit?"

The wary look came back. "Last time I sat, you . . . kissed me."

Clarissa watched Bo's eyebrow quirk as he shot her a harmless gaze. As if he could *ever* be harmless. "I was wondering if we were going to talk about that," he said.

"We're not, definitely *not* going to talk about it," she assured him. But she sat because her heart was pounding so loud, she couldn't hear herself think. She leaned her head back and closed her eyes.

"That's fine," he said. "Then we can talk about the other."

"The other?"

"About why your brother terrifies you."

Her eyes flew open and she sat straight up. "Where did you get that idea?"

He smiled, but it was a sad smile. "I'm crippled, Clarissa. Not mental."

Suddenly unable to sit, she leaped back to her feet. "I can't do this, Bo. And don't—" She whirled on him, pointing her finger at his chest. "Don't you flash those incredible eyes and ask me if it has anything to do with your damn chair, because it doesn't, and after that k-k—"

"Kiss?" he interjected, mischief lighting up his expression.

"Yes, fine, kiss. We kissed. We *really* kissed."

"You think my eyes are incredible?"

She rolled hers, then slapped her forehead. "God save me from men!"

Bo laughed, reached for her, but she evaded him.

"No. Bo, I'm sorry. I've got to go."

Arms pumping, heart racing, she took off down the windy garden path, for the second time that day using her mobility against him as she ran top speed, dodging through the plants so he couldn't possibly keep up.

Bo sat at the edge of the mat in The Right Place as Jeff worked with Michael. With Michael's mother watching the proceedings, a worried frown on her face, Bo struggled to keep his own face impassive.

It was difficult. They'd gotten nowhere with the boy in the six months they'd been working with him, and this scared Bo. At five years old, Michael had such a long life ahead of him, they simply *had* to get through.

Jeff leaned over Michael, smiling as he tickled his tummy. Michael closed his solemn, too-old eyes and slowly turned away.

Clearly frustrated, Jeff glanced up at Bo. When Jeff picked Michael up and put him back into his wheelchair, Bo glided close. "Hey, bud."

Michael, limbless except for his right arm, stared down at his one hand, which lay limp in his lap.

Bo leaned in so that no one could hear what he said. "Want to talk?"

As was typical, Michael didn't respond, though Bo and everyone else in the room knew darn well he could. There was nothing mentally wrong with him; his injuries were purely physical. He just refused to accept his situation.

"I know you hate this," Bo said quietly. "Believe me, I know."

Michael lifted his head and stared at him with big black eyes. In them Bo saw fear, hopelessness, and the death of such simple dreams as running across the grass with the sun beating on his back.

Something deep inside Bo cracked open, and things he'd been keeping back, hiding from himself, emotions too painful to deal with, spilled out. What had happened to Bo was unfair, criminal.

But he'd lived twenty-five years before his own tragedy. This boy, who'd also been in a car wreck, had not even gotten a little of that.

"I wanna go home," Michael said quite clearly, and Bo's agony increased even as excitement stirred.

He'd *spoken*.

A quick glance at the boy's mother told her she was as startled and as excited as he.

"I know you'd rather be home," Bo told Michael. "But you've got to work your body, got to keep it in shape. It's dangerous for you if you don't. Your body needs attention, Michael, just like your mind does."

"I got no body."

The boy's gut-wrenching reply had Bo's throat thickening. His eyes burned. Even Jeff, hardened to some extent by the horrors he'd seen, blinked rapidly.

"Oh, Michael," he said. "Yes, you do have a body. And you have an arm, and your right hand." Bo clenched that hand in his. "With it, you can learn to do so much. We can show you."

"It's *dumb*. My chair is dumb." Michael reddened suddenly as he stared at Bo's chair.

"It's not fun," Bo admitted. "But if I didn't use this chair, I'd have to lounge around in bed all day. And everyone knows there's only *dumb* television on during the day. How boring would that be?" While he spoke he worked Michael's good arm, massaging and manipulating. He worried at how thin it was and how little the boy had used it.

As he worked he kept up a one-sided chat with Michael, hoping for another response, but he got nothing.

Out of the corner of his eye, Bo caught sight of that strawberry-blonde hair. Clarissa came to the edge of the mat and stayed respectfully back. He knew she was there because she was next to see Michael, to work on fine-tuning the use of his hand, but he liked to believe she'd showed up five minutes early for a glimpse of him.

Yeah, right.

But Bo breathed in her scent, took in the comforting sight of her smile, and he dreamed. Dreamed about her slim body bowed over him in pleasure, her hair falling over his bare chest as she rode him . . . *Not* productive thoughts, he told himself sternly as he felt his body react.

With a struggle, he gave his full attention back to Michael.

"Are you ready to do this yourself?" Bo asked. "Ready for some work?"

Michael's full lower lip came out. "I wanna walk."

"Let's start smaller," Jeff suggested with a smile as he held up a small rubber ball. He pressed it into Michael's hand. "Let's squeeze this together."

Michael had eyes only for Bo. "You have legs."

"Yes."

"I don't," he said.

"I know, bud."

"I want legs."

God. "Michael—"

"Why don't you use them?"

"Because they don't work so well," Bo said, his chest tight. "In fact, at the moment they don't work at all." His legs were still cramping painfully from the merciless workout he'd subjected them to the night before. But cramps, agonizing as they may be, were worth their weight in gold because he could *feel*. Yeah, without aspirin, the pain would bring him to his knees, but it didn't matter. Pain equaled feeling, and he'd take it any day over the alternative.

Over Michael's alternative.

"I can't play basketball," Michael said out of the blue. At this, his face crumbled. His tough attitude disappeared, and he sniffed as his eyes welled.

"Wanna bet?" Bo smiled, his heart light for the first time since two nights before in Clarissa's garden. "I can teach you."

The hope that flared in the boy's face was priceless. And Bo intended to keep it there.

But then Michael shook his head.

Jeff hunkered close. "He's telling you the truth, Michael. Bo runs this center. But he's also the sports director. He organizes all kinds of sporting events for people in wheelchairs. People just like you. And you know what?" He grinned. "He's specializes in basketball. Want to know why?"

For the first time Michael looked at Jeff.

" 'Cuz he's the best," he told him in a conspiratorial whisper as together they stared at Bo. "He beats the pants off me every time we play. Want to watch us sometime?"

Michael, caught up in the magical offer, nodded. Bo grabbed a basketball and smiled at Michael. "Chuck that little pathetic rubber ball back to Jeff, would ya? Let's play some real ball."

This was the real test, and every adult in the room held their breath at the small ball in Michael's hand. He hadn't used his arm of his own free will since the accident.

Michael glanced down at his hand.

Bo leaned forward and gave him an encouraging, casual smile. "Go on. Get rid of that thing."

But Michael hesitated, clearly uncertain.

Jeff patted his shoulder. "Come on, bud. Give it a try."

After another moment of the boy's painful indecision, Clarissa spoke up from the sidelines. "That's all right, Michael. If you don't want to, we'll just go on to our appointment. Practicing with your spoon. Much better than playing with a silly old ball."

Michael hated working with the spoons. Bo could have risen and kissed Clarissa on the spot, because she had given Michael exactly the nudge he needed.

The boy sucked in a breath and rose to the challenge. Lifting his right arm, the arm he'd let atrophy over the past months, he sent the small ball flying toward Jeff.

It sailed all of two feet, but by the wild, loud cheers that erupted from everyone present, it might have gone two miles instead.

Grinning, Bo dribbled his basketball. Then he passed it off to Jeff, who dribbled several times before sending it back to Bo.

Michael soaked up each and every movement.

Bo picked up Michael's hand and continued the dribbling, letting Michael set the ball in motion.

And Michael did something he hadn't done since his debilitating accident. Something everyone in the room had assumed they'd never hear again.

He *laughed.*

Bo thought it was the best sound he had ever heard.

But then Clarissa laughed too. When he looked at her, stunned by the unfamiliar sound of her joy, he saw that her eyes sparkled bright with unshed tears. He winked and she laughed.

Now *that*, Bo decided, was undoubtedly the sweetest sound he'd ever heard.

SEVEN

"Married yet?"

Bo groaned, dropped his head to his desk, and resisted the urge to throw the phone against the wall. "No, Dad. Fresh out of brides at the moment."

"Now, son . . ."

His father had perfected that injured tone of voice years before. It was a leftover from his years as a defense attorney, and it never failed to leave Bo soused with guilt. "Sorry. Everything okay?"

"Yep. Your mother's just—"

"Worried. Yeah, I know. She's told me at least sixty times this week. Look, Dad, don't take this personally, but you have plenty of other children to bother. Why me?"

His dad, always good-natured, laughed. "Okay. I get the message."

"Good. I gotta go." But affection had him relenting. "I love you, Dad. Now don't call me back until tomorrow."

"I'll try. Love you, too, son."

Bo hung up and sighed.

He couldn't imagine getting married, sharing every day of his life with someone who would probably resent his hours, bug him about how many nights a week he played basketball, and nag him about hanging up his clothes.

Unless the woman had light strawberry-blonde hair, a sweet smile, and a heart of gold that she protected with an impenetrable brick wall.

Unless it was Clarissa.

The days flew by for Clarissa. One week into her job, the weekend loomed ahead of her, and things seemed so unexpectedly good.

Stop it, she reminded herself. Of course things are good. The rest of her life was going to be good. And if she discounted the fact that somehow her brother had managed to find her, everything had gone right on track.

She hadn't called Sean back, and she wouldn't. It brought her unbelievable pain even to consider ignoring her own brother, but she had to.

She wanted to remain safe. Free.

She smiled into the silent, empty kitchen of The Right Place, her eyes lingering on the blank wall over the table the employees used for their meals.

Bo had asked her—twice—to paint a picture for that space. She could easily imagine a river scene, with a lovely cottage on the shore and a bridge under which ducks swam happily. But the thought of *her* painting resting there only brought panic.

Her art seemed so personal, so representative of the inner feelings she kept from the world. She simply wasn't ready for strangers to look at it.

"Excuse me."

Instinct had her stomach leaping into her throat at the deep, unrecognizable male voice. In the small kitchen, where she'd been gathering her things to go home, Clarissa turned and faced the tall, dark-haired man she'd never seen before. "Yes?"

"You're Ms. Woods."

"Who are you?"

He neither smiled nor held out a hand, both of which put Clarissa further on guard. Instead he moved closer, effectively blocking her off between the refrigerator and the wall.

She had no way out. Unless she wanted to brush past him, which she didn't.

"I'm Michael's father," he said curtly. "Walter Wheeling." His eyes narrowed, and his already grim mouth tightened to a thin line. She noticed a muscle spasming in his cheek. "I wanted to talk to you about his progress."

Which would have been fine, except for the way he stood blocking her way out of the room.

He purposely used his large body to intimidate her, which both annoyed and scared her. She was well used to such tactics; her husband had been a master of them.

"I'd be happy to talk to you about Michael," Clarissa said with a brave smile she hoped didn't wobble. Familiar old fears and insecurities came flying back. "But this area is off-limits to anyone but employees, and I'm not the person in charge of Michael's care—"

"Excuses. All I ever hear is more frigging excuses." His closed fist slammed down on the table, making her flinch.

They stood so close, she could see the rage and pain shimmering in his eyes, and it was the latter that gave her strength to remain standing. "Mr. Wheeling—"

"I pay a fortune for Michael's care," he bellowed. "And I can't get answers!"

"Mr. Wheeling, you really need to speak to—"

"No. *You're* here and *you're* the person I want to talk to." The veins in his neck bulged. "You're the one I'm paying a fortune to try to teach him to eat. Well, doc, he's not eating!"

"I know." As always when upset, her southern accent gave her voice a rough twang. "But it takes time—"

"Tell me why the hell my boy can't use his hand, a perfectly good hand, to pick up a damned spoon and get food into his mouth?"

During his temper tantrums, which Clarissa suddenly had reason to suspect were hereditary, Michael had taken to throwing or flinging his food. But that had been *before* this week, *before* the breakthrough Bo and Jeff had made with a basketball. From Michael's chart, and short conversations with his mother, she knew this man was a truck driver, and rarely at home. Was it possible he hadn't heard?

Shaking in her shoes, Clarissa spoke quietly, slowly, giving him time to absorb her words, praying it would be enough. "We're making terrific progress, Mr. Wheeling, just in this last week. You should see him now—"

"Are you not listening to a word I'm saying?" His voice rose still higher as he took yet another step toward her, leaving less than two feet between them. With the refrigerator grinding into her hip and the wall at her back, Clarissa had to bite back her automatic scream.

He looked so terrifyingly angry.

"I want answers!" he yelled.

Clarissa nearly swallowed her tongue. Some small, rational part of her brain knew she was safe, knew that if she screamed, any of a dozen staff members would race in and assist her, but the rest of her didn't care. Everything inside her shut down, simply closed off, leaving her incapable of speech, unable to cope. She closed her eyes and started to tremble.

"What is going on in here?" came a familiar, husky voice, sounding unusually stern.

Clarissa had never been more happy to hear anyone in her life. Her eyes flew open, locked with Bo's warm, dark ones, and unexpectedly filled.

Bo's face flushed with anger as his gaze whipped from Clarissa's to Michael's father.

"I want answers!" Mr. Wheeling shouted again.

"Walter." Bo's words were kind, despite the tension that held his body rigid. "Please, sit. You look like you need a break. Come on, now. Sit."

The man, so huge and menacing a minute before, drew a ragged breath.

Bo pulled out a chair. "What's this about?"

"We were discussing Michael," Mr. Wheeling said, subdued now by Bo's willingness to listen. "I'm unhappy with the progress."

"I see." Bo guided his wheelchair around the table, effectively forcing Walter back a few steps, away from Clarissa.

Clarissa, who'd felt as though she were suffocating, gulped in a greedy breath of air. Through her shock, she watched Bo work magic on a rage she couldn't face.

"If you have a problem with any of my staff, Walter, you should take it up with me, okay?" Bo's gaze, completely honest and open and caring, never left the man. "There's no reason to scare Clarissa half to death."

Without warning, Mr. Wheeling crumbled into the closest chair and covered his face with his large, oil-stained hands. "I'm sorry," he whispered. "I'm just so damned helpless to fix this. I can't make it better for him and it's killing me. I didn't mean to yell at her. I just can't take this any longer."

Bo made a sound of acceptance, of understanding. "Michael's okay." He squeezed Mr. Wheeling's shoulder. "He's doing terrific."

"Really?"

"Really. He's doing far better than you appear to be doing."

Walter dropped his head to the table. Sobs erupted from him; horrible, agonizing sobs that shook his frame. Clarissa's vision wavered as tears stung her own eyes.

She'd failed, miserably.

Knowing that, she left Walter to Bo and quickly made her exit.

Once in the parking lot, she hesitated. She knew she didn't have the presence of mind to attempt driving, and she didn't have her keys anyway, so she headed around the outside of the building and ended up in the small grove of trees in the back. There, beneath the tall palms, with the faint scent of salty air, Clarissa sank down on a wooden bench, pulled her knees up until she could hug them close to her chest, and dropped her head down.

It had finally happened. She'd finally allowed her past to affect her work.

She should have understood Walter was lashing out in order to ease his own pain. She could have helped to defuse it. She'd been trained to do so, and that she hadn't been able to help really humiliated her.

Bo would fire her now, and she deserved it.

Above and around her, night continued to fall. From a hundred yards off came the soothing sounds of the pounding surf. The moon was full, splashing silver beams of light over her.

She liked it here, wanted so badly to make it work.

"Clarissa."

She jerked, snapping her head up. *Bo*. Her pulse raced at the sight of him. He sat in his chair, several feet away from the bench. She could tell nothing of his thoughts behind that impassive face.

"You okay?" he asked.

Good question. Easy question. It was the answer she couldn't figure out. Especially when asked so . . . distantly. "Yes."

He just stared at her. A chilly breeze blew his hair over the collar of his forest-green polo shirt. Something flickered in his expression, something she couldn't quite catch.

"I'm sorry," she said abruptly, for the first time in her life choosing to handle a confrontation rather than run, which was what she *really* wanted to do. But the thought of Bo being upset with her unnerved her more than she could have thought possible. "I handled that badly in there."

"Why?"

Something was wrong, she could feel it. Sense it. Where was the warmth she'd counted on from him? Where was her solid, giving anchor? "I don't know—" she started, but he shook his head, anger flashing.

Anger at *her*. Another first.

"Don't lie." He spoke with a quiet hurt that sliced deep. "I don't want to know you can do it so smoothly."

She was a master at lying, always had been. It had been a survival tactic. So had retreat, which she was considering right this minute. But running would gain her nothing except an appointment at the unemployment office. Not to mention the loss of what was rapidly becoming one of the most important relationships in her life.

"Do I scare you?" he asked suddenly. His voice was low and anxious, and not the impassive one he'd used only a moment before.

"No. No, you don't."

He looked relieved, then suddenly wary. "Why not?"

"Why not? That's a silly question. You just don't."

He hadn't moved, still stayed away, and she

wondered why. He'd certainly never kept his distance before.

"On the surface you're tough," he pointed out, almost to himself. "I'll give you that. But I'm beginning to understand it's all a great big facade. You're really afraid of your own shadow. You jump when someone looks at you cross-eyed."

"Bo—"

"You nearly fainted tonight while facing an angry, distraught parent, though I *know* you had training for exactly that." His gaze stayed steady on hers, making looking away impossible. *"Men* scare you, Clarissa. Yet *I* don't. Why is that?"

His terse tone put her on edge. She got up, and would have walked away, but he grabbed her hand and held firm.

Ice Queen, Ice Queen. Dirk's favorite taunt reared up and bit her. She choked back the bitterness.

"What?"

Oh, God. She'd said it out loud. "Nothing. *Nothing."*

"You're *not* an Ice Queen." His fingers tightened on her wrist. "Who called you that?"

"No one. Let me go."

"Why don't I scare you, Clarissa?" While Bo waited for her answer he stared at her face, willing himself to relax. But the quick flicker in her gaze, how it shifted ever so slightly over his unmoving legs and chair, chilled him. "Never mind," he said harshly. "I already know." He swore softly, then let her go, and because he didn't trust himself to speak, he turned away.

He heard her first few running steps from him and closed his eyes. The coward, he thought. She's going to take the easy way out. Again.

But she surprised him. He heard her stop, hesitate. Her soft steps coming close warned him, then she was hunkering down to his level. "Bo."

"Leave me alone, Clarissa."

"But—"

"Go."

Her eyes were huge and wide in her face. At her throat, her pulse beat frantically. "Bo, please."

He shook his head sharply, then because he couldn't possibly keep it inside, he let the fury go. "You're not afraid of me," he said as calmly as he could with his heart pumping his blood as if he were a steamroller going uphill, "because I'm not a threat to you."

She sat back on her heels. "Of course you're not."

He should have let her run. Anything would have been better than facing this. "Because in your eyes, I'm half a man."

"No! Bo—oh, dammit." She sank down to the bench, tipped her head back, and stared up at the dark sky. She blinked unseeing at the twinkling stars. Her slender body was curled upon itself on the bench, her hands fisted. An unhappy pose, to say the least. She looked as if her best friend had just died.

Anger warred and lost to compassion. Calling himself every kind of fool, he wheeled to her.

"I don't think of you as half a man," she said to the sky before he could speak. "I never thought that. But God help me . . . you were right about the other. I refused to think of you as a real person. One with normal wants and needs."

The renewed anger was expected, but Bo was totally unprepared for the hot ball of hurt that burned all the way down to the toes he couldn't feel.

"From the very beginning, I didn't want to notice you as a man," she said in a low, quiet voice to herself. She swallowed convulsively. "I thought that because you were in the chair, I had nothing to fear."

"You *do* have nothing to fear," he said, bitterness blocking his windpipe, so that it burned when he talked. "I would never hurt you, Clarissa. With or without the damn chair."

"I know," she whispered. "Or at least I tell myself I know. But it's still so hard." She pierced him with a look filled with pain and suffering. "I've made you angry."

He shook his head.

She made a noise of disbelief. "Yes, I have." She squinted in the faint light as she studied his eyes. "You're still angry."

"No. You hurt me." He took her hand, pressed it in his own.

"Why? Because I can't give you what you want?"

"You have no idea what I want," he assured her grimly. "If you did, you'd run screaming from these woods, believe me."

She tugged her hand free. "I'm sorry if I've let you think there's something between us. There's not."

"I can see that."

"I just want to work with you. And be friends," she said.

Friends. He'd heard that one before, far too many times. It was the ultimate blow-off and he knew it all too well. "Sounds exciting."

Clarissa was still pale, but lifted her chin in an endearingly dignified way that made Bo's gut clench. "And I'm sorry about the way I handled Mr. Wheeling. I hope you'll give me another chance."

She'd withdrawn, right before his eyes, which had his anger exploding again. He kept it to himself this time because there was no way he was going to beg her. He didn't need the heartache, thank you very much. "I'm not going to fire you." He backed his chair up and wheeled onto the path. "We waited too long to get help as it is."

He nearly burned rubber off his wheels when he skidded away.

Later, at home, he couldn't decide which hurt worse—his heart, or the blisters on his hands from his reckless race away from her.

EIGHT

Clarissa painted all weekend. Luckily she'd never been one to need a lot of sleep. A throwback, she knew, to the nights she'd lain awake, plotting her escape from a tyrannical father. Then, years later, she'd done the same with her husband.

Her brother didn't call again, a mixed blessing. Now she lived with a new fear. If he'd found her, he would come see her.

If he did, and her father got out of jail, then he could follow Sean and find her as well.

Just the thought brought on a new wave of panic so great she couldn't breathe. On Monday morning, she went to work and tried to block such thoughts from her mind.

After two appointments, Sheila caught her in the hall.

"What's the matter?" she demanded, leaning

on her walker as she eyed Clarissa with a probing gaze.

"What could be the matter?"

Sheila gave her a long glance. "Oh, please. You're jumping at your own shadow. You drill me daily about any personal calls, yet other than that one anonymous call last week, no one rings for you."

"Maybe I don't like telephones."

"Then why are you biting your nails down to the quick? Spill it, Clarissa."

All her life she'd yearned for a best friend, a true best friend that she could "spill it" to. But she'd never had one, mostly because of her own fear of allowing someone close to her. "I don't know what you're talking about."

Sheila looked disappointed. She reached out and gently touched Clarissa's face, her finger running lightly over the dark circles of stress and fatigue she knew lay beneath her eyes. "You look so unhappy. Just like Bo does. Both so hurt."

Clarissa stiffened and Sheila made a little noise of compassion that nearly undid her. Sheila lifted her shoulders. "I just want it to work out, that's all. The two of you deserve it."

"He . . . said something to you?"

"No," Sheila admitted. "But I can tell something happened. He nearly killed himself Friday night in the gym, and I imagine he'll do it again tonight."

"What do you mean?"

Sheila shifted her walker and started down the hall. "Why don't you go find out?"

Another challenge.

Clarissa sighed and went to her next appointment. Tina, a six-year-old stroke victim, had been left with shunts in her brain. The entire time Clarissa worked with the girl's hands, her thoughts raced.

If she went to the gym that night, as Sheila had obviously intended, what would she find?

"Why isn't she responding?"

Clarissa glanced up. It was Tina's mother, a small, angry woman she knew most of the therapists tried to avoid. "She is," she said calmly, stroking Tina's arm in reward when the girl's hand clenched around a toy. "See?"

Mary Martin's eyes flashed, and in them Clarissa saw so much more than anger. "That's not good enough," the woman insisted, her petite body shimmering with tension and grief and the burden of raising a handicapped child. "I want her to be able to feed herself."

"She can't do that until she can learn to control opening and closing her hand," Clarissa told her, her heart cracking at the pain behind Mary's rage. She saw it all too many times, parents unable to accept their child the way he or she was. "We're getting there."

"It's not fast enough!" the woman cried. "I want more. You're not doing enough to cure her."

Clarissa knew there was no "cure," but knew

also that Mary wouldn't believe it. "Tina is really doing wonderfully, Mrs. Martin. She can reach out and touch now, see?"

But Mary refused to look. She came closer to Clarissa, then closer still, until they were eye to eye. "I'm going to go to your supervisor," she threatened, the tears just behind her anger evident. "I'll get you fired. You're not doing anything for my baby!"

Clarissa's heart tightened, not at the threat, but with worry for both Tina and her family. At her mother's raised voice, Tina started to whimper in her throat. Clarissa smiled reassuringly at the child while speaking to her mother in a quiet, soothing tone. "Mrs. Martin, please. If you could just wait until this session is over, I'll be happy to take you to my supervisor and we could talk this out."

"I want to do it now!"

In tune to her mother's raised voice, Tina screamed, a high-pitched, hurtling scream. Waving her extremities and tossing her head about, she closed her eyes tight and kept on wailing.

Mrs. Martin stared at her, horrified, her aggressive stance dissolving. "Oh, my God. Did I do that to her?"

Clarissa gathered Tina in her arms and, murmuring over the screaming, began rocking her back and forth. When Tina's mother opened her mouth, Clarissa shook her head sharply and kept murmuring to the frightened, shaking child.

Mrs. Martin closed her mouth and sank to the mat. She covered her face with her hands and wept. When Clarissa had Tina quiet, she set her back into her chair.

"Here, sweetie," Clarissa said, handing Tina her favorite toy—a huge, red ball. "Hold on to that for me, will you?"

Then she turned to Mrs. Martin. Sinking to her knees, she touched the woman's arms. "Are you all right?"

"No," came the muffled reply. "God, I'm sorry."

"You know about our support group for parents."

She nodded.

Clarissa knew Mrs. Martin had refused to join it, saying she was fine, well-adjusted, and needed no one's help. "Maybe it's time. What do you think?"

Mrs. Martin sighed, sniffed, and nodded.

Clarissa knew an overwhelming relief. It'd be so much better for Tina if Mary learned to cope. Smiling gently, she looked up . . . and met Bo's gaze.

She hadn't heard him come in.

Neither of them smiled; there was too much between them. In light of that, Clarissa couldn't have explained why she felt so breathless and tingly. Her stomach did a slow somersault. Her palms went damp.

For the rest of Tina's session, Clarissa was painfully aware of him.

"You did great," he said quietly, gesturing with his head to where Tina and her mother sat together on the mat. "That was a rocky situation at best." His eyes warmed and her stomach fluttered. "And I'm proud to have you as part of this team."

Ridiculous to be so affected by his praise, but knowing it didn't stop the pleasure from flowing through her like a warm spring breeze. "Thanks."

He stretched his shoulders, as if suddenly uncomfortable, and turned away.

"Bo . . ."

He whipped around so fast, his chair didn't even squeak, his expression filled with dark hope. "Yeah?"

Oh, God, she didn't have the words, she just didn't. "Nothing." She watched the hope fade before he turned and left, wishing she could call him back. Wishing she could take back what she'd said the last time they'd spoken.

Truth was, she'd never been more aware of a man in her life. He was gorgeous and masculine and full of more sexuality than she knew what to do with, but it went far deeper than that.

She supposed that was what terrified her the most.

Before she could blink, she found herself chasing after him, breathlessly catching up with him in the hallway, just outside his office.

He simply went in, waited politely while she followed him, then folded his hands.

Clarissa bit her lip as the door shut behind her, shutting her inside the office with him. "About the other night," she said in a rush. "I'm sorry I hurt your feelings. I didn't mean to."

"I know." But his inscrutable expression didn't ease.

"Bo—" She had absolutely no idea what to do or say. And maybe some of her helplessness showed, for he sighed.

"Forget it, Clarissa. I think I understand."

"You do?"

He hated that he did; after he'd thought about what it had all meant, his fury had quadrupled, though not at Clarissa. He'd thought of little else since that night. "I watched you just now, dealing with an irate parent. She was every bit as upset as Mr. Wheeling was, but you didn't fall apart. You didn't get the shakes. You didn't look or act in the least bit terrified." He paused meaningfully and she paled. "Not like that other night."

Clarissa looked nauseated. She backed to a chair against the wall and sat.

It was difficult to rein in all his feelings, but he made the effort because he didn't want her to think he blamed her. "Was it your brother? Is that why you're avoiding him? Or your husband?"

She brought a hand up to her lips, as if to hold in her words.

"Which one of them hurt you?" he asked

softly, his heart tight with the knowledge that her fear came from memories. That she used those memories as a wedge between them.

She had closed her eyes. "Am I so transparent, then?"

"Oh, Clarissa." Sick to the depths of his soul, he moved to her. "I care about you," he said carefully.

"You do?"

"Of course." More than she would ever realize, he thought. "But what you're looking for—a relationship without any of the kick—it isn't enough for me."

"Without the kick? What does that mean?"

"You want it easy." He took her hand, stroked the stiff fist. "You want compassion, kindness, patience, and you deserve it. But you also want no waves. You want the coffee without the caffeine, the roller-coaster ride without the speed. You want the love without the passion, Clarissa." Unable to help himself, he cupped her jaw. "I can't give it. I want the whole thing, and I won't settle for less."

Her entire body was tense. She pushed him away. "I never said I wanted anything from you except a job." But her breath caught when he leaned forward, his thumb stroking her lower lip. He kissed her softly, savoring the touch and lingering for a minute, and her body betrayed her with a tremble he knew damn well wasn't fear.

"All right," she admitted with an explosive

sigh when he backed off. "I lied." She shocked them both when she cupped his face in her hands. "I'm so tired of being afraid, Bo. I'm tired of not feeling." She leaned close so her words whispered over his mouth like a caress. "Make me feel again. Put your mouth back on mine and kiss me like you mean it."

He didn't think he could handle that *and* maintain his stance of resisting her. "Clarissa, that's not what you need—"

Her eyes flashed in the first sign of temper he'd seen her show. "Don't tell me what I *need*, Bo. I've had a lifetime of being told that. I know my own mind, and I can act on it. This is what I want."

"But—"

"Oh, just be quiet," she snapped, and yanked him closer, crushing her lips to his.

He might have resisted even her, but when he felt her incredible body pressed against him, pride and resolve flew out the window. All that mattered was getting closer, tasting and feeling as much as he could. But after her initial aggressiveness, Clarissa paused, and the hesitant way her hands clenched on his shoulders, the unschooled way she held her mouth to his, squeezed his heart.

"It's all right," he murmured, dragging his mouth from hers to taste her neck. "Doesn't it feel good?" He drew a small patch of her skin between his teeth, sucking and nibbling his way to the pulse that danced wildly at the base of her throat.

"Bo . . . I can't breathe."

"Just draw in air, sweetheart. And forget thinking, just for now." He certainly had. He still understood that they had no future, but she tasted and felt too good to hold back, and he'd starved himself too long. His hands skimmed down her sides and up again. Down and up, so that the heels of his hands just brushed over the sides of her breasts. She moaned and tipped her face back up to his, meeting him in another hot kiss.

Just that quickly, he had to have more. He plundered her mouth while his hands, shaking now, smoothed up over her ribs and cupped her firm breasts.

A sound jangled his senses, and he wasn't sure if it was Clarissa's startled gasp or the harsh ring of the telephone. He broke away, pulling back. She stared at him, lips wet and swollen, looking wide-eyed and sexy as hell.

The phone rang again and Clarissa leaped to her feet, tugging her blouse down, which only emphasized her hard, rosy nipples thrusting against the thin material.

His pants were suddenly far too small. "Clarissa—"

"Your phone . . ."

He wheeled to his desk, but thankfully whoever it'd been had hung up. He glanced at her across the room. "Clarissa—"

She made a soft sound of distress, then ran to the door, grabbed the handle. Suddenly she went still, not looking at him. To the door, she whispered, "That was . . . nice."

"Nice." Bo laughed softly and rubbed his eyes, thinking if it'd been any *nicer* he might have exploded right then and there. "Yeah."

"I mean, it didn't—well." She swallowed hard. "It felt good, is all." She ducked her head and studied her shoes, and Bo wished he could see her expression and know what she was thinking.

He rolled his chair toward her.

"It's never felt like that before," she said, clearly confused. "There was only my husband and he . . ."

"He didn't bring you pleasure?"

"No."

Quite an admission. What she left unsaid told him a lot. His heart constricted, then expanded, until his chest ached at that flash of innocence he'd sensed in her before. Innocence and an unleashed passion burning just beneath the surface. He'd barely touched her and she'd nearly gone up in flames in his arms. He wanted more. He wanted it all.

"It just felt really good."

The marveling wonder in her voice nearly undid him. "Look at me, Clarissa." Her gaze met his. "It should always feel . . . really good," he said with care.

She flushed bright red and opened the door.

"Wait. Are you all right? I mean, are you safe to go home alone? If you won't tell me anything about your fear, at least let me know that much."

"I'm safe," she said, and shut the door softly behind her.

Bo waited until later to try to relieve some of his frustration. Alone in the building, he wheeled onto the basketball court, dribbling a ball at his side.

Forty sweaty, agonizing minutes later, he'd succeeded in relaxing a bit. So much so that he was feeling good, confident he could do anything. Even walk.

He wheeled down the hall to his office, grabbed his leg braces, and wheeled back to the empty court.

It took him a few minutes to get himself strapped in. Then, with a sudden surge of strength and undeniable need, he shoved up from the chair and pushed it away. He willed his right foot to shift outward so he could step.

Nothing happened.

He used his hands, bending slightly at the waist, to push his leg out. But he wasn't quick enough to straighten, and he hit the wooden floor hard enough to send stars dancing through his head.

The noise his metal-and-leather leg braces made as they connected only further humiliated him, but he had so exhausted himself, he couldn't move to save his own life, not to mention he hurt like hell. It made his mortification all the more complete, he thought, lying winded on the wood floor.

He couldn't have been more wrong.

The gym door opened, making him groan out loud.

He hadn't locked it.

The woman who'd been on his mind, the last person in the world he wanted to see him like this, came into the room. "Bo, I've restocked—*oh, my God.*"

She took one look at his pathetic, crumpled form and ran straight to him. "Bo!"

Painfully aware of how he must look, Bo reverted to locker-room language and swore the air blue. "You ever hear of knocking first?" he demanded.

Pale, she dropped to her knees. "It wasn't locked. Thank God."

"Don't."

But she reached out and touched him, concern and fear on her expressive face.

It was more than he could take. "Clarissa—"

"Shhh, don't talk. Not until I see how badly you're hurt."

"*Don't,*" he repeated. His breath heaved, his muscles trembled violently from the workout he'd subjected them to. He couldn't move, dammit, and nothing, *nothing* could be as bad as this.

"Oh, Bo," she said, her hand on his stomach, which immediately clenched at the touch. "What happened?"

"Nothing."

"*Bo.*"

"I'm testing out the hardness of the floor with my body, what the hell does it look like I'm doing?"

Her lips tightened.

He might have said more, might have kept yelling at her, but he couldn't hold back his wince as a sudden razor-sharp cramp shot up his thigh.

"Where is it?" she asked calmly, but her breath hitched when he winced again. "What did you hurt?"

She'd grabbed his shoulders, and when he rolled, trying to shake off the stabbing pain, she went with him. He grimaced, embarrassed to his very depths. Again he closed his eyes so he wouldn't have to face her pity. "Get out." His voice was hoarse with agony and humiliation, but he couldn't control it.

"But—"

Arrows of pain shot up his hip from his graceless landing. He'd wrenched his elbow. None of it compared with the hurt deep inside. "You don't want to mess with me right now, Clarissa. Get the hell out."

NINE

A man's fury. She had good reason to fear it. Clarissa stared down at Bo sprawled beneath her and wrestled with her demons. Though he would never know what it cost to face him down, she did.

"I'm not leaving."

But before she could do anything more, Bo's face twisted, wrenched by agony, and any conscious decision was taken from her. He became a patient, *her* patient.

Determined to see if he'd broken anything, she reached out to run her hands down his legs. But the leg braces, which she'd never seen on him before, got in her way.

Before she could remove them, Bo slapped her hands away and snarled at her. "Don't."

"What were you doing?" she fussed as she leaned over him, worried about his pallor.

"The Irish polka." Shifting, he groaned. "Damn." He stiffened when she tried to touch him again. "Go away, Clarissa," he gasped when he could draw a breath.

"And leave you to your misery?" she demanded. She managed to start to unstrap him.

"Back off."

"No." One brace came off. Her fingers searched for, and found, the cramp in his thigh.

He moaned, then gasped with relief when her fingers tightened on his leg, rubbing on the series of knotted muscles she found there.

It took him a minute to catch his breath. "I'm not in the mood for this," he finally said between clenched teeth.

"Makes two of us. But I have no intention of leaving you here." When she finally sat back, her fingers brushed against the hard, ungiving sinew in his upper arm, reminding her how deceiving strength could be. "How bad is it now?"

He let out a violent expletive in a dangerously quiet voice that would have had her quaking had she not been so worried about him. "Bo—"

"Go. God . . . just go."

"Let's get you up."

"Damn you!" He rolled away from her, giving her his back. "Leave me alone."

He lifted up slightly on his hands, but not much. Clarissa realized he couldn't push to his knees if he couldn't feel them, and though she made a living out of helping people, she'd never felt more sympathy for anyone in her life. What it must be like for this virile, otherwise healthy athlete to be unable to walk—it must kill him. The muscles in his arms strained to hold his weight. His shoulder and back muscles, outlined starkly by his sweat-dampened T-shirt, trembled visibly.

She would have sworn earlier her heart was dead, but it couldn't be if it hurt so much. "Bo—"

He sank back and dropped his head to the floor. "I'll fire you," he swore. "If you don't leave."

She lifted an eyebrow in surprise, but even she knew the venom was directed at himself, not at her. "You already told me you wouldn't."

"You're hovering over me like a mother hen, and it's annoying as hell."

She could tell by the way he had held himself up on his forearms that he hadn't hurt any of his upper body, at least too badly. But she didn't know about the leg he hadn't let her touch, and feared he couldn't feel if he *had* injured it.

She had to weigh that possibility against the more critical, more obvious injury to his male pride. It didn't take a genius to decide a tactical retreat would be the best recourse, but it would be hard to leave him, knowing he probably couldn't get up by himself in his weakened condition.

"All right," she drawled softly, rising to her feet. "I'll go. But I'm not leaving the building until I know you're out too."

He swore again, but she said nothing, just

walked to the door of the gym as slowly as she could, hoping he'd call her back.

He didn't.

The next day, Bo watched Clarissa come in the front door. She eyed him carefully, but said nothing, for which he was grateful. He'd acted like a jerk the day before, and knew he had to apologize, but for some reason, the words stuck in his throat.

Sheila shot him a questioning look as Clarissa said hello to her, not Bo, then walked by. Not nearly as reserved as Clarissa, she jumped right in and spoke. "What did you do?" she demanded, looking at him, eyebrows high, arms crossed.

"How do you know it was me?" Guilt tore at him.

"Honey," Sheila said, drawing out the word, "when a woman ignores a man like Clarissa just did you, it's *always* the man's fault."

Later Bo decided that if Clarissa could forget what had happened, so could he. Besides, he wasn't sure he trusted himself to get close enough to talk to her. He'd decided they weren't meant to be, but that didn't mean he didn't want her—he did. More than ever.

But when Clarissa ignored him the entire day, it couldn't be put off any longer.

He found her in the kitchen, singing under her breath to the portable radio on the counter. He grinned at her technique of humming through the words she didn't know as she prepared a bowl of oatmeal, which she used to teach Michael to spoon up to his mouth. Occupational therapy, in which the therapist concentrated on small motor skills, had never particularly drawn him before. He preferred the sheer strength physical therapy required. But despite how mixed-up he felt about Clarissa, he loved to watch her work.

The way she drew out her patients, coaxing more from them than they would have guessed they had, amazed him.

"Hello," he said.

While she didn't jump at his voice—an encouraging sign in its own right—she didn't so much as spare him a glance either. Definitely not the kind, caring Clarissa he'd come to know.

He glided his chair up next to her and flashed the smile that had been used to charm many a female. "You sing pretty."

"Hmmph."

A tough cookie, he thought, amused. "I couldn't carry a tune if you put it in a sack and handed it to me."

She didn't so much as crack a smile.

"You ready for Michael?"

"Mm-hmm." The little whipping motions she was making with her fork in the oatmeal had her hips swinging slightly. His eyes feasted on the movement before slowly roving up over her trim torso. Exactly at his eye level came her breasts, small and firm. Even now he could remember how soft and giving they felt in his hands, how they'd tightened instantly into two delicious peaks he'd wanted to taste.

He shifted in his chair as, once again, his pants seemed to shrink.

Clarissa ignored him.

He cleared his throat and was thankful she didn't so much as glance at him, because he couldn't possibly have hidden his erection in the sweats he wore. "There's a tournament tonight," he said. "An adult one. Sheila and I are playing. You coming?"

Eyes glued to the bowl of oatmeal, she lifted a shoulder noncommittally.

Oh, boy. She was really giving him the treatment. "We always go out for pizza afterward."

She added more water and kept stirring.

Dammit, he shouldn't have to grovel. She should take his apology professionally. There was no reason to drag this out with silence. So he'd screwed up and yelled at her, and he was sorry! Anyone could see that. "With Jeff and Sheila's antics lately, it's a guaranteed good time."

"You going to miss your nightly torture session for that?"

No doubt, anger became her. Her eyes, flashing brilliantly, finally lifted to his. Color made her cheeks rosy. And her mouth . . . God, her mouth. He wanted to kiss it until it softened beneath his. "Is that yes you'll come, or no, Bo, you can go to hell?"

"Both." She turned back to the sink and effectively dismissed him.

Grudgingly, he admitted to himself that a *real* apology, with the actual words, might be unavoidable here. Since he'd acted like a first-class jerk the night before, he supposed she deserved it.

"Ah, about last night . . ."

"Forget it," she said succinctly. She put the bowl on a tray with a couple of spoons and a sipper cup filled with apple juice—Michael's favorite.

"I think we should talk about it."

"Why?" She blinked her cool eyes at him. "So you can shout at me again?"

Okay, so she had an ego, too, and he'd stomped on it. But dammit, didn't she understand how hard it had been for him? He'd felt so helpless, so exposed, and he hated that. "I'm sorry."

"Sorry that you nearly killed yourself without a thought as to how people who care about you would feel? Or sorry for shouting like a baby afterward just because you knew you were wrong?"

"Um . . ." Oh, hell. She wasn't going to let this go. "Both, I guess." He cocked his head. "You care about me."

She lifted the tray and glanced at him with disdain. "You're in my way."

"Admit it. You care."

"I never said so, did I?"

"Yes, as a matter of fact, you just did."

"Oh, for Pete's sake—*excuse me*."

He didn't move. "Look, you caught me at a bad moment. Being spread out like a flopping fish doesn't bring out the best in me." He took a huge chance and, reaching up, took the tray from her, carefully setting it down on the table. Then he slipped a hand around her waist. "I never let people see me like that, Clarissa."

The look she gave him wasn't full of pity, as he'd half expected, but exasperation. "You can't walk, Bo. It's a fact. It's nothing to be ashamed of. Everyone has something they can't do, something that makes them feel vulnerable, and quite frankly, being around the children you are with every day, most of whom are far worse off than you, I'm surprised you haven't learned that by now."

Bo realized it hadn't occurred to Clarissa that last night he'd been trying to *walk*, and he purposely didn't enlighten her. First, ridiculous as it seemed, he was afraid to jinx himself, and he was determined he *would* walk again.

And second, he wasn't ready to face her reaction.

"What makes *you* vulnerable?" he asked, his voice low and unintentionally husky. His hand curled around her waist, loving the feel of her, wishing for more. "What is it *you* can't do?"

"I can't be—" She bit her lip and shoved his

roaming hand away. "I can't believe how you do that. I actually almost told you."

"Come on," he coaxed. "You've seen me at my worst; now let me see you." He could see the indecision on her face and tipped the scales in his favor. "It's only fair."

"Oh, all right," she snapped. "If you must know. I can't be . . ."

"Yes?"

"You wouldn't understand."

"You can't be what?"

A sigh escaped her. "I can't, you know. Be, um . . . intimate." She closed her eyes and made a sound of regret, grappling with him as he tried to hold her hand. "I can't believe I told you that." Again, he slipped an arm around her, which she tugged at. "Now let me go."

"We've already been pretty intimate, sweetheart." He thought of her drugging kisses, of her sweet moan of passion when he'd touched her.

"But we didn't get . . . You didn't—" She backed up, leaped for the tray as if it was a lifeline. "Oh, I don't want to do this. Not now." Ignoring him, she took a step.

"Clarissa, I—"

"*Stop.*"

She stood there, holding the tray, trying to avoid his gaze, trying to look tough, but he saw the uncertainty and embarrassment lingering. As if she didn't quite trust him not to turn on her unexpectedly. Or laugh at her. "The Ice Queen," he said softly.

She stiffened.

"You're not." The woman had managed to give him more erections in one week than he'd had in the last five years. "My God, Clarissa. You can't really think that of yourself." But he saw that she did.

"I'm going to be late for Michael." She was clearly mortified. "Now to use your own words, *back off.*"

"You'd throw the words of a man in pain back in his face?"

"You bet," she assured him. "Now move it or you'll be wearing apple juice on that pretty face of yours."

He grinned. "I knew you cared about me."

She groaned.

"Clarissa?"

She was at the door, and barely paused.

"When do I get a painting for this wall?"

"Why do you want one?"

She looked so leery, he had to laugh. "Because you're good, that's why." Her leeriness turned into doubt and he sobered. "Is it so hard to believe I think you're good? That I want to show off what you can do?"

"Yes," she whispered, and just that quick, she was gone.

The intercom buzzed from the front office. "Clarissa." Sheila's voice called into the room, obviously assuming she was still there. "Line two, hon."

She clicked off before Bo could tell her Clarissa was long gone. Shrugging, he wheeled over to the wall unit, mounted low enough for him to reach it easily. "Hello?"

"Yes, I was looking for Clarissa Woods," said a polite male voice.

With *anyone* else, he wouldn't have thought twice. But this was Clarissa. Sweet, *terrified* Clarissa. "Who's calling?"

There was a short pause. "This is her brother, Sean Abbott. Is she there? It's very important."

Bo wasn't about to confirm Clarissa's whereabouts. "You've called before."

"Yes. She hasn't returned my calls. Has she gotten them?"

He knew it was none of his business, but he couldn't help himself. "Maybe you should stop calling her."

"Look, please, just tell her I called again. Tell her if she doesn't call me back, I'm coming to talk to her."

Bo stared at the telephone when it disconnected.

"That," he said to no one in particular, "sounded like a threat."

By the end of the day, Clarissa felt pleasantly exhausted. She'd go to the tournament because she'd promised. After that, she looked forward to an hour or so of painting, then falling into bed.

Hopefully, her night would be dreamless. Peaceful. They had been lately, and she knew she had her new life to thank for that.

A small part of her could acknowledge it went even deeper. That she had a specific someone to thank for it, but she wasn't ready for that.

She couldn't possibly admit to herself that she'd actually caught herself daydreaming about . . . It seemed so embarrassing really. So silly. But she'd actually been thinking about how Bo had kissed her. How he'd touched her, creating a paralyzing sort of pleasure. A pleasure she wanted to feel more of.

He had wonderful hands. Wonderful arms. A most wonderful chest. And the most wonderful thing of all was his mouth.

Crazy. That explained it, she'd gone crazy.

She sighed and pushed away the unfamiliar romantic thoughts.

The parking lot was well lit, but the air was chilly, so she hurried, her breath coming out in white puffy clouds. She jingled her keys, already thinking about the colors she wanted to use on her canvas tonight.

"Cold enough for you?"

A startled scream escaped her lips and her keys went flying. Three feet away sat Bo in his chair. "Bo!" She put a hand to her chest. Beneath her fingers her heart drummed against her ribs. "Don't do that! You scared me."

He didn't smile, didn't apologize. His wayward hair fell over his forehead as he studied her. "I waited for you."

"Why?"

"Because I couldn't let you go alone. You got another call today, Clarissa. From Sean."

She felt the color drain from her face.

Bo glided closer, bent, and scooped up her keys. Silently he opened her door and pushed her down into the seat, wheeling close so that their knees touched. He took her hand, peering worriedly into her face. "He said if you didn't call him back, he's coming to you."

A half sigh, half groan came from her. *Great.*

"Okay." Roughly, he spoke again. "That's it. Let's call the cops. They can—"

"What? *No!*" She pulled her hands back from him and rubbed her face. "You don't understand."

"Then tell me."

"Sean isn't a threat." She struggled with an explanation. "I'll call him back. He'll stay away."

"If he's not a threat, why would you want him to stay away?"

How much to tell him? Nothing, she decided when she looked into his tense, battle-ready face. Absolutely nothing. "Sean won't hurt me," she whispered. "He's my baby brother."

"Are you sure?" He was clearly torn between

the desire to rip the words from her and trying to remain patient.

"Of course."

"But you look so frightened. Why can't you trust me enough to tell me what's the matter?"

Trust wasn't something she was prepared to offer, not ever again. "I have nothing to fear from Sean," she said finally. "You're just going to have to believe that."

Night sounds surrounded them. Crickets singing shrilly, ocean slapping against sand. Palms rustling. "I'd believe anything you told me," he admitted. "I just wish you'd tell me more."

"There's not too much to tell."

"I have a feeling you're wrong about that."

Because he looked so worried, she forced a smile. Thanks," she said softly.

"For what?"

"For . . . you know. For caring."

He searched her face for a long moment. "You don't have to thank me for that, Clarissa. Just get used to it."

TEN

At Bo's insistence, Clarissa ended up riding to the tournament with Sheila. The minute she walked into the local high-school gym, the years peeled away. Something about the smell and sounds, she supposed. Sweaty bodies and the pounding of rubber soles against the wood-plank floor.

Only this time, in this game, the sounds were different. It was the screech of the wheelchair wheels stopping and starting on a dime. The occasional clink of metal as two chairs collided.

She sat with Jeff and Sheila and prepared to suffer through the games, since she couldn't very well admit she secretly hated basketball.

Well, what she *really* hated was the memory of Dirk glued to the television while she did her best to remain completely silent during the broadcast. It was always the same, and for as long as Clarissa lived, she'd never understand the man she'd been married to. A sports nut, he needed to be totally absorbed in each game, yet he always required her presence. He took perverse pleasure in making her sit next to him, frozen, afraid to breathe because he'd forbidden her to make any noise, to move so much as a muscle.

And she'd been so afraid of the possibility of him turning his anger on her that she'd followed his every impossible wish.

Clarissa closed her eyes for a moment and reminded herself that that part of her life was over. Forever.

The stands on either side of the court were brimming, all eyes glued to the center, where the action had just begun. She had to talk, had to say something, just to prove to herself she could. "This is an annual event?" she asked Jeff.

He didn't growl, didn't seem to regret the interruption in the least. In fact, he grinned. "Yeah. Last year this building was closed for repairs and we had to have the tournament outside. It was drizzling, but no one would have missed it. Do you like to play?"

"Oh, no," she said with horror before she could stop herself.

His eyes narrowed thoughtfully. "Not much of a fan, huh?"

"Not really," she admitted.

"This evening will change that," he said with typical male confidence that any sport was the answer to a woman's prayers.

Clarissa's eye was drawn to Bo, down on the court. He was strong and sure and a magician with the ball as he wheeled and handled the play.

"He's a wizard," Jeff said, noticing her reaction. "He could have gone pro if he'd wanted."

She thought of what Bo told her about the pressure his family and friends had put on him, how, ironically enough, the accident had relieved him of it. "Maybe he didn't want to."

Jeff shrugged. "I'm just glad he uses his talent now, because he's truly amazing."

"You mean in coaching?" She couldn't seem to help but ask, though she was afraid to learn too much about the man who had begun to fascinate her more than any other man ever had.

"Yeah. He says he gets far more joy out of that than playing, and since he could have played if he'd wanted to, I have to believe him."

Clarissa couldn't help but think Bo had made the right decision. If he'd gone pro, then lost the ability to play because of the accident, he might never have recovered.

Clarissa had no idea what she had expected as she watched, but it hadn't been to sit enthralled for the next two hours, afraid to go to the bathroom because she'd miss something.

There were four coed teams in the county, all put together by Bo. She watched, mesmerized, as two of the teams were eliminated, leaving two to fight it out for the championship. Bo and Sheila played on one of these teams.

"Bo's won every year for the five years he's been doing this," Jeff told her.

"You'd think they'd switch the players around to make the teams more even."

Jeff laughed. "They do. But whichever team Bo is on always wins. He even tried bowing out one year, to make the play more fair. But everyone demanded he come back. They all love him."

She could imagine why. Bo was the type to inspire deep loyalty. All the players were in wheelchairs, including Sheila, who couldn't possibly have played with her walker. Clarissa loved watching the receptionist, calm and warm and so kind by day, turn into a man-eating machine. She was ruthless on the court, shouting obscenities and insults.

But Bo, he was beautiful. He moved with fluid grace as he dodged his chair in and out of the play, his quick rhythm setting him apart from everyone else. He wore dark basketball shorts, a matching tank top, and an expression of fierce concentration. The other players wore the same uniform, but none of them looked as good. His chest was broad, his arms toned and primed, the muscles defined with effort and sweat. And every time he did something to his satisfaction, his intense face broke out in a cheeky grin.

"Want to come to the stands with me and get something to eat or drink?" Jeff asked.

Bo covered his man—or in this case, woman—weaving in and out, then in again. He grabbed the ball, a cocky yet apologetic grin breaking out as the woman stuck her tongue out at him. Executing a neat spin, he wheeled across the court and sent the ball flying . . . and, with a swish, scored.

The crowd erupted.

"No, thanks." She grinned at Jeff and admitted, "I don't want to miss anything."

In the next few minutes, Bo's team took the game and the championship. Clarissa, inwardly shocked at her lack of inhibitions, leaped to her feet with the rest of the crowd and cheered her delight.

"Thought you didn't like basketball."

She looked at Jeff. "Well, the excitement got to me, that's all."

"Uh-huh." He slanted her a knowing glance. "Come on, I've got something to show you."

He brought her down to center court, where the players, drunk with success, were hugging and congratulating one another.

"You've converted her," Jeff said to a very satisfied and exhausted-looking Bo. "She's hooked."

Bo looked at Clarissa and something passed between them. Something unexpected, something . . . hot. Clarissa took an involuntary step backward and crashed into someone.

She whirled, apologizing profusely to the man in the chair she'd so clumsily bumped into. "I'm sorry—" Before she could finish, the crowd surged, bumping her backward yet again, and she took another blind step for balance.

Without warning, she stumbled into someone else, but before she could turn, she was grabbed around the waist and tugged down.

She landed on that someone's sturdy lap. Hard.

"Oh!" she exclaimed, wriggling, twisting.

"Relax," Bo said as his gentle arms encircled her. "I've got you now. In fact, I think I'll claim you as my trophy."

She looked into his face and opened her mouth to retort she was no man's prize.

Before she could, his mouth fully and unerringly took hers.

The crowd erupted again.

"I came with Sheila. I can go home with her," Clarissa said firmly a short time later. She and Bo stood in the quickly emptying parking lot of the high school. She was still desperately struggling for dignity, and recovering from that amazing kiss he'd given her on the court.

He, on the other hand, looked as if nothing had happened. He'd showered and put on a clean pair of sweats and a T-shirt, and looked disarmingly gorgeous.

She'd never get used to that, looking at a man and purposely considering his looks. But Bo did something to her, something she wasn't sure she was ready to identify. "Where's Sheila?" she asked, sounding a bit desperate.

"She's going for a victory pizza." Calmly, Bo unlocked his Bronco, holding the passenger door open for her as she climbed in.

"Maybe I want a victory pizza too," she said, lifting her chin and ignoring his patient face.

"So I'll call for one."

"You don't know what I want on it. Maybe I like anchovies and yogurt and pickles."

"In that case, we'll get *two* pizzas."

"Why are you doing this?" From her vantage point in the seat, she could look down at him where he still sat in his chair, holding the door. "I mean, I don't understand. You said you didn't want me, remember?"

"I never said I didn't want you," he told her, rampant desire chasing the amusement across his face. "I said I didn't want a relationship that wasn't whole, that didn't go both ways." His look intensified, heated. "Because believe me, Clarissa, I want you, more than anything."

She had the insane urge to look down past his face to his lap, to see if what he said was true. This inexplicable, primal need so shocked her, she gasped out loud. "But I don't want you back."

"Is that why you stared at me while I was playing basketball? Is that why, when I pulled you down on my lap, you wriggled around until you felt my reaction—which by the way, took less than two seconds?"

She blushed and looked away. "I didn't stare at you. And I never *wriggle*."

"Another lie." He sighed. "I thought I'd cured you of that."

"Bo—"

"Look, Clarissa," he interrupted, a little crossly. "There's something between us, I know you feel it."

"No."

"And I know it scares you," he said with sudden gentle seriousness. "Hell, it scares me, too, because I know you're not ready for this. Which pretty much leaves me in a position I hate—vulnerable."

Despite his handicap, it was difficult to picture this virile man vulnerable. Turning away, she studied the night sky through the windshield as her thoughts raced.

"Are you going to hurt me, Clarissa?"

Her head whipped back to face him and his grim smile. "Didn't think about that, did you?" he asked. "But it's true. I care about you, even though I didn't want to, and because of that, I've handed you a great power." His gravelly voice made her stomach tighten. "Be kind," he whispered.

"Oh, Bo." She looked back out into the night, which he apparently took as her getting ready to bolt.

"We both know if you run away from me now, I can't chase you." Bitterness tainted his voice, as he was clearly frustrated with his immobility. "But believe me, if I could, I'd hop up there, scoop you up, and prove to you once and for all what I've said is true." He leaned as close as he could with both his chair and the door of the Bronco blocking him. "And just so you know, it would be more than 'good.' There'd be no pain involved. No force." His voice went husky now, raw with need.

A sound escaped her, a mix of denial and hunger. She bit her lip to keep silent. To keep from begging him to show her what he meant. But she wasn't ready. Around them, the lot had just about emptied. She knew Sheila would be long gone. "Are you going to take me home?"

He had one arm braced on the door of the vehicle. The other was on the edge of her seat. His head dropped down between his shoulders. As she waited for him to speak she stared at the crown of his head, at the swirls of deep brown hair falling in random waves.

She remembered how perfect Dirk's hair had always been, without one strand out of place. Stop it, she demanded of herself silently. That would be the last comparison she'd allow herself to make.

Just the thought brought a measure of relief.

"We have to talk," he said finally, his fathomless eyes meeting hers.

"We already did."

"About your behavior."

She'd heard that one in her past, and before she could mask it, she felt a flare of nerves and fear. At the same time Bo reached up and took a hold of the shoulder seat belt she hadn't yet secured. At the sight of his raised hand approaching her face, all logic fled, and instinctively, she ducked away from him.

He froze, then swore. Slowly, deliberately, he put her seat belt on and dropped his hands to his chair. "When are you going to get it?" he asked, his voice raw, his eyes hot. "I'm not going to hurt you. Ever."

Without another word, he turned and wheeled around the Bronco. In silence he dismantled his chair, then hauled himself up into his seat.

Because Bo didn't trust himself to speak, he flicked up the radio until soft rock filled the interior, and he drove into the night. In his own abject misery and fury it didn't occur to him how she might feel about coming to his house at night. Not until he'd parked in his driveway.

He turned to her in the darkened car and tried to read her stony expression. "This is where I live. Alone, unless you count Tabitha."

"Your latest kidnapping victim?"

He grinned, pleased with her sarcasm. "Wait until you meet her," he said, his teasing tone making her blue eyes narrow in suspicion. "She's sophisticated, sleek. Incredibly beautiful."

"Really," she said dryly, turning away.

"And she's crazy about me." He was thoroughly enjoying himself now. "Every night she stretches out next to me, refusing to let me leave until I stroke her into oblivion."

Her lips twitched, telling him she was onto him. "Something you'd be good at, I imagine."

"Yeah. Want me to show you?"

"Definitely not."

He chuckled.

"You don't really expect me to believe you have a cat."

"Of course I do.

Her jaw fell open. "Really?"

He'd expected her to get mad at him for teasing her, or at the very least to laugh at herself for starting to get worked up, maybe even a little jealous. But this incredulous, wide-eyed look of wonder stunned him.

"Do you really have a cat?" Her voice was a whisper now, a hushed, reverent tone. "And you care for her? Oh, Bo."

All amusement fled in the face of this overwhelming rush of emotion. *God*. He'd have to watch his step, because this woman staring at him as if he were the most wonderful man on earth was about to have him falling head over heels for her.

And she didn't even know it; she had no idea of what she did to him. "She was a gift from my sister after my accident." Without allowing himself to think, he unhooked Clarissa's seat belt and drew her toward him. His fingers brushed her hair back, played in its silky strands. "Do you mind telling me what is so amazing about me having a cat?"

"Men don't like cats."

He laughed. "Wherever did you get that idea?"

In his arms, she stiffened. She fell silent, staring out the window at his house.

"Clarisa, we need to talk. Come inside with me."

Her fascination with staring out the window instead of at him was frustrating, but he said nothing more while she decided.

"Remember when I told you what I couldn't do?" she asked eventually.

As if he could forget. "That you can't be intimate?"

Nodding, she bit her lower lip. "Did you believe me?"

He chose his words carefully. "I believe that *you* believe it."

"Can *you?*"

"Can I what?"

"You know . . . can you be intimate?"

A laugh escaped before he could stop himself. To his shock, he felt himself reddening. "Ah, yeah. Yes, I can."

"I thought so," she said with great disappointment.

"Clarissa," he said with another choked laugh. "You have a way with words."

Then, as if she just realized how she'd sounded, she bit her lip harder. "Oh, God. I'm really making a disaster of this." She wrung her fingers together and stared at his house. "It's a very big place, isn't it? I suppose that's because it's all one floor. How many bedrooms—no. Never mind." With this, she covered her face with her hands. "I should have gone for pizza," came her muffled voice just before she inhaled deeply, letting it out with an audible sigh.

He hated to see her so nervous. "Why don't you just say what you want to say, Clarissa," he suggested gently.

"Okay." She lifted her face and looked at him. "I don't want to . . . you know, try to be intimate."

Since this was nothing new, Bo could think of no reason why disappointment flowed through him.

"But if I did," she added with a sweet whisper, "it would be with you."

ELEVEN

Somehow Bo got them out of the car and up the ramp to his front door, though it was difficult with his vision clouded by a mist of desire so thick, he could hardly breathe.

He got a handle on it, barely, because he had to. Clarissa trusted him enough to come into his house and there was no way he would jeopardize that trust. No way at all.

But sometimes he resented the cumbersome wheelchair, regretted he hadn't made more headway on his braces and walker, because he would have given anything to be standing as he led her into his home.

Stupid male pride, he knew, but he couldn't stop it.

You can't walk, Bo, Clarissa had told him the other day. *That's a fact. It's nothing to be ashamed of.*

Everyone has something they can't do, something that makes them feel vulnerable.

How he wanted to stand up and shout, you're *wrong!* I *can* walk! I *will* walk! Instead, he had to bite back his tongue and bide his time, because deep down he feared she might be right.

He couldn't walk, not ever again.

"What are those bags?"

At Clarissa's question, he looked down and saw the four plastic grocery bags on his porch, filled to the brim. He groaned in frustration.

"Bo?" In an unusual show of affection, she touched his arm. "What's the matter?"

Bo was thinking he'd have to put all the food away before he could talk to Clarissa, and he had to talk to her before he could grab her and kiss them both blind. "Hell," he muttered. "Those are my groceries."

"On the porch?"

"I have them delivered from the market twice a week."

"Oh." Sympathy filled her lovely eyes and he gritted his teeth as his frustration grew. Maybe the groceries could wait. So could their talk. Maybe he could just tug her back into his lap and convince her to wriggle again. Then he'd kiss her, really kiss her, and she'd say she'd just been kidding about that intimate stuff not happening and—

"I never thought about it," Clarissa broke in, still looking sympathetic. "It must be hard to manage both your wheelchair *and* the food cart at the store."

"No, I just hate grocery shopping." Seeing her embarrassment, he had to laugh. "I hated it far before my accident, Clarissa. They've been delivering for years."

"Oh."

Together they lugged in the bags and dumped them in his kitchen. "Leave them," he said, and led her into the living room. He didn't care if everything spoiled, he was determined to get past Clarissa's barriers. Tonight.

The minute he flicked on a lamp, a small meow sounded. A solid black streak launched at him and he braced himself for the four-point landing that usually involved claws in his lap. When he grunted at the impact, Tabitha pushed her head against his chest insistently, demanding to be touched.

"Just like a female." But he ran his hand over her obligingly, smiling at the rough purr.

Clarissa smiled too. "I thought cats were haughty and stingy in their affections."

"No, that's you," Bo pointed out, chuckling when Clarissa stared at him, startled. Suddenly she laughed.

"Love that sound," he murmured, looking at her.

She went tight with tension and straightened as she pointed at him. "Stop that. Stop that right now. No come-ons," she reminded him.

"No come-ons," he repeated. Not yet, he thought. He transferred himself and Tabitha from his chair to the couch, where Clarissa surprised him by sitting close. She slid a hand along Tabitha's back. Ecstatic to be with people after a day alone, the cat tipped over and stretched out on her back, purring loudly.

"She's so pretty."

Bo couldn't think past the way Clarissa's hair tickled his arm, how her light scent tormented and teased. Her eyes, fixed on the cat in his lap, were bright and lit with pleasure. Her skin glowed and he longed to lean forward a few inches and taste her freckles.

Clarissa tickled Tabitha's exposed belly for a few silent moments before turning her head and lifting a clear, wide gaze on him. They were so close, he could move an inch and stroke her mouth with his.

"Don't forget," he warned in a whisper.

She didn't move, except for her eyes, which ran over his lips. "Forget?" she asked breathlessly.

"You wouldn't want to accidentally seduce me, not if you can't be intimate."

Her breath caught, but she still didn't move. "Why am I here?"

Slowly he lifted a hand from Tabitha and touched Clarissa's cheek. "To tell me why you're still resisting my obvious charms."

A corner of her mouth quirked. "Haven't you ever been resisted before?"

His fingers stroked her jaw, sank into her hair. "Not by someone who means so much to me."

"Bo—"

He halted her words with his fingers. "No," he whispered, dragging a thumb over her full bottom lip until her eyes went cloudy. "No temper. No tough words to hide your emotions. No sarcasm. Just me and you, and the truth. Please," he added in a voice that had gone ragged with need and hunger. "I deserve that, Clarissa."

Her head dipped down, and he gave her a minute, lazily petting Tabitha. Clarissa drew a deep breath, then started speaking, her southern twang thickening as she did. "I had a kitten once. My brother found it stuck in a tree, scared and frightened. He gave it to me because it was my eighth birthday." Her hands shook as she reached up and restlessly smoothed back her hair.

Bo took them in his larger, warmer ones, dislodging Tabitha, who with an insulted mew, got up and stalked off, tail high.

Clarissa's eyes closed. "I loved that kitten on sight."

He could feel the terrible tension in her as she straightened away from him. His body responded, and his hands went to her shoulders to knead some of the knots he felt there. "My father had forbidden any pets, and when he found her cuddled up on my pillow, he . . . he threw her across the room, breaking her neck against the wall."

Horror slashed through him, and he went still. "Did he hurt you, Clarissa?"

Clarissa's head was down, studying her hands. "All the time. The kitten was just another excuse."

There weren't words for the violent rage that hurtled through Bo. He needed to hush her, needed to haul her close and never let her go.

But as if she'd opened up a huge dam with her words, they kept flowing, pouring from her in an unstoppable torrent, and he could do nothing but hold her and listen to the nightmare that had been her life.

"I tried so hard to be good, to make him love me like he did Sean, but I couldn't. I ran away and ran away, but because the laws weren't all that great back then in Texas, they always brought me back to him. I left the day I was eighteen and filed a restraining order to stay safe."

"Where is he now?"

"Prison. He, ah, got in a fight with a coworker. The guy died."

Bo had no idea what to say; it was difficult to think rationally with so much adrenaline inside him. But Clarissa wasn't done breaking his heart.

"I met a man a couple of years later." She dropped her gaze again as if ashamed of this. "I had avoided men until then. He sort of . . . dazzled me. He was one of my college professors."

Bo closed his eyes and fervently hoped the guy had been a prince.

"Dirk seemed so kind and caring compared with my father. So confident and sure of himself. I agreed to marry him because I couldn't believe a man so perfect could want me. *Me*," she added with hushed awe. "The entire time we were engaged, he was a complete gentleman, and I was so happy. I was a virgin—" She blushed profusely. "And he never pressed me. We waited until our wedding night." She paused, winced, then whispered, "He turned out to be a control freak. He never hit me or anything, he didn't have to. I was already so easy to intimidate. He liked that. He liked to manipulate me with my own fear."

"Did he hurt you in bed?"

She wouldn't look at him. "Before we got married, he used to kiss me. I liked that." She flushed as if that were something to be ashamed of. "But things changed after we married. He never kissed me. And I never . . . liked anything he did to me after that."

It'd been a long time since Bo had felt like crying and smashing something at the same time. He clenched and unclenched his fists, wondering how the hell he was supposed to remain calm and collected when he needed to pound something.

"I thought at first it was my fault—" She stopped, startled, when Bo made a choking sound. "I left him just before he died."

So frail yet so strong, he thought, and from somewhere he managed to find a way to speak. "Tell me you killed him. Please tell me that."

Clarissa's smile held no amusement, only pure spite. She loved to say this. "His girlfriend's father did."

"Good enough."

Clarissa pulled back slightly to get a good look. His expression was fierce, rage burning in his eyes. Rage and sorrow, a deep, haunting sorrow. She imagined him slaying dragons in his wheelchair. For her. For some reason that image made her vision waver as her eyes stung with unshed tears. "God, Clarissa. What you've been through."

The burning in her throat deepened, and she couldn't see past her tears. She blinked rapidly, trying to understand why she felt like crying, here, now, when it was all over with, and had been for so long. "I've never told anyone before, but I had to tell you. I know you're waiting for me to get used to you, waiting and thinking that the time will eventually come, but it might not. I want you to understand that. It might never come."

"Oh, sweetheart."

"I mean it," she said, desperately struggling not to lose it in front of him and further humiliate herself.

He reached up and tucked a strand of hair behind her ears. "Did you like it when we kissed?"

"Yes, but—"

"Did you like it when I touched you?"

She closed her eyes. "Yes."

"Then you'll like the rest. I promise."

She wanted to believe him so badly, but the years of repression were difficult to overcome. More, she'd never made the first move on a man in her life. How did she get him to show her all he'd promised?

He pulled her close. "I won't rush you."

She wanted to be rushed, dammit.

"Never," he promised.

It was too much, his caring voice, his warm arms. A sob erupted from her throat, and she could no longer hold back.

"It's all right," he whispered. "It's all right." Without warning, his arms banded around her tightly. She couldn't move, couldn't breathe.

And it didn't matter. For the moment she couldn't think of anywhere she'd rather be as she burst into the tears she'd been holding back for so many years she couldn't count. She felt her chest heave as the force of her crying shook her, soul-baring cries that came from deep within.

Bo didn't say a word, but just held her tight, stroking her back and hair, rocking her gently against him, and she shuddered with the strength of the storm raging through her. His hands were warm and firm, and she knew he'd never let her go. Unless she wanted him to.

She had no idea how long they stayed that way, with her crying until her head felt it weighed a thousand pounds. But a liquid languor affected her bones, and exhaustion eventually crept in.

Still, she couldn't release him, didn't want him ever to stop holding her.

Turning her face into his chest, she clung. "Don't let go," she said thickly as her mind drifted.

"I won't, I promise," he vowed, and those were the last words she heard as she fell into exhausted slumber.

Clarissa awoke with a start, her chest unbearably heavy. The reason became immediately apparent when she reached up in the darkness and found Tabitha sitting on her, calmly washing her face with a delicate paw.

She'd fallen asleep at Bo's place. Shooting straight up, she dislodged the cat, who let out a disgruntled meow.

A pair of long, warm arms wrapped around her. Bo's arms. Bo's wonderful, safe arms, and though they were hard with strength, she welcomed them.

"Come back here," he murmured, his voice husky with sleep, and she realized they'd fallen asleep together, tangled on his wide, comfortable couch.

Her throat felt thick with the tears she'd shed, her eyes puffy. But Bo tugged her gently down, hushing her as he tucked her back against him. "Okay?" he whispered, and she felt so okay, she threw her arms around his neck and hugged hard.

Now, she thought. *Let him show me all my aching body wants to know.* Hugging Bo was different than anything she'd ever experienced before. Because they were lying side by side, and because his legs stayed heavy and still on the couch, she didn't get that terrible claustrophobic feeling she expected. It was . . . wonderful; drugging, but not claustrophobic.

"This feels nice." Her voice sounded muffled against his neck, but she didn't pull back because he smelled so incredibly good, fresh from the shower of the gym.

"Don't sound so surprised." His cheek rubbed against the top of her head. "The rest is even better."

She was counting on it.

He stretched, reaching above them, and suddenly, with a click, a lamp's soft light filled the room. Humor glittered in his eyes as he set his hands on her upper arms, slowly and gently lying back as he pulled her over him.

Her hands fell to his chest as she held herself up on that broad, hard wall of muscle, and she gasped at the contact.

He reached down to straighten his legs beneath her sprawled ones. Because he was huffing a bit, and struggling, she helped him until he settled back.

But then his huge, gentle hands were urging her back down on top of him, pulling until she lay with her legs entangled in his still ones.

She stared down into his face, her hands gripping his shoulders in painful fists, her breath hitched in her throat, more aware of him as a man than she'd ever been.

"Relax," he murmured, rearing up to kiss her nose, "we're just going to lie here."

No, she wanted to cry. *Show me. . . .*

"Now, why don't you remind me why you think you can't be intimate." His hands, slow and easy, stroked up and down her stiff arms.

She held herself off him because her mind told her she should, but her body had gotten a taste of his hard, warm one and wanted another.

His eyes were dark and soulful, and so intense. "Your pace," he promised.

Dammit. She wanted . . . God, she wanted, and had no idea what to do. Swallowing her embarassment, she said, "I've done this before and—"

"We can fix that." Now purpose gleamed in those eyes as his hands ran down her arms to her hips. A quick, gentle nudge brought them in perfect alignment with his, where she was forcibly reminded that he could indeed function as a man.

"Oh, my," she said weakly.

Encircling her waist with his arms, Bo brought her lower, closer. As he gazed into her eyes her heart gave a nervous kick against her ribs. "My heart's going a mile a minute."

His lips curved as his eyes misted. His voice sounded husky with emotion. "That's the first time you've admitted to having a heart." He drew her down even closer so she could feel his heart's steady beat against hers. "How does it feel now, Clarissa?"

She closed her eyes. "Like it's going to leap right out of my chest."

"Come closer," he whispered, a hand nudging on the small of her back. "Just a little, sweetheart."

She'd forgotten, completely forgotten, that he had little to no mobility in his legs, but realized it now as hers lay shifting restlessly over his unmoving ones. Without thinking, she did come a little closer, and the moment she did, his lips brushed hers. They were warm and receptive, and slightly parted as they hovered close, barely touching her.

Her eyes drifted shut.

"This is good, isn't it?"

Always before, she'd felt trapped. Dirk had never taken any pains to arouse her during sex and the thought of it now made her tense. But she was on top now, and for the first time in control. It made a world of difference. "Am I up here because you want me to feel in charge?"

"You're on top because I can't be." He emphasized each word with an openmouthed kiss along her throat that had her eyes crossing with lust. "And because you're going to like being in control. It'll feel good, I promise."

"Okay." She felt so breathless. "Don't take this the wrong way, but—oh!" She gasped as his tongue darted out and danced along the pulse point at the base of her neck. "I think I like it up here."

She felt his lips smile against her skin. "I thought you might."

His concern for her comfort touched her all the more because she knew how difficult it was for him to admit his own failings. She didn't say more because at the touch of his mouth on hers, all thoughts faded into pleasure. She loved the feeling of him sprawled beneath her, loved knowing his uneven breathing was because he found her desirable.

Power, she thought with amazement. She held the power, and she liked it. A lot. "Yes," she agreed with a wide smile. "This is really nice."

His smile was wry. "Maybe later you'll decide this was even better than 'nice.'" Again his lips lightly grazed over hers, barely touching, leaving her yearning for more.

"This is intimacy," he whispered against her mouth, his hands gentling her. "No force. No pain. No helplessness. Just you and me and what we feel for each other. Okay?"

At his soft words, she relaxed even more.

"It's the most wonderful thing a man and a woman can share, and this is it." As light as a caress, he nibbled her lower lip. "Do you like it?"

"I—" He continued to tease her with his mouth as she fumbled for words, just the barest of touches, making her emotions and senses leap to life.

Just as purposely, he pulled back, opened his eyes, and looked at her, heat smoldering in his gaze. "Clarissa? Do you like it?"

Like it? She wanted more. Take it, she told herself. She dipped her head back down, and holding his face between her hands, she claimed his mouth.

He immediately lifted her up and away, slipping his hands into her hair to hold her head and pull her back. To her shock, she heard her own moan of disappointment.

His soft laugh washed over her, then he rewarded her with another barely there caress of his lips. Then another, and another, as his tongue teased the corner of her mouth.

It was wonderful, delicious, and the rest of her resistance, if there was any left, melted away with her bones as she slumped over him. He never stopped the baby-soft kisses and a liquid yearning seized her. She leaned into him harder, needing, wanting. He closed his mouth against her.

Frustrated, she pulled back, and was again rewarded as he closed his lips gently over hers, tracing the outline with his tongue.

She moaned and he turned his head away.

Frowning, frustrated, miffed beyond belief, she sat up, straddling him without any concern of repercussions.

He blinked up at her innocently.

"What are you doing?" she demanded, her hands on her hips.

He laughed and tugged on a lock of her hair. "Playing hard to get. Is it working?"

"Is it working—you mean, you're dodging my kisses on purpose?"

"Yep."

"But, I don't understand. You want me." Sitting directly on him as she was, his erection nestling in the cleft between her thighs, there was no way she could she miss his excitement.

She wiggled a bit, just to make sure, and watched his eyes go opaque, heard his muffled groan. "You do," she said. "I can feel that you do."

"There's no hiding it," he agreed in a rough, thick voice that brought a shiver of anticipation down her spine.

"So why won't you kiss me right?" she demanded, and again he laughed softly.

"I *am* kissing you right. Right into insanity. Don't you like it?"

"I want more. I want the rest." She wanted it so badly, she shook with it and he hadn't even touched her yet.

"Is that what you think intimacy is? Intercourse?"

"Well, yeah."

"You're wrong." Reaching, he flipped off the light. His arms came up, and once again tugged her down. "Come here, Clarissa, and I'll show you."

TWELVE

It took Bo a minute of concentration and a series of grunts and a shifting of his heavy, unmoving lower body, but he eventually lay on his side, cradling Clarissa against him, his arms loosely around her.

A second later four heavy paws landed on Clarissa's hip. Tabitha gave her an indolent glance before settling down right there to wash herself. Outside, the wind blew. Against the windows branches of pines brushed and swayed.

Inside, a calm settled. Clarissa touched Bo's face, running her fingers over the day's growth on his chin, smoothing the crease between his eyes, stroking the mouth she yearned for.

At her touch, his hips rocked against hers once, pressing his heat and need against her. She returned the movement. A thrill shot through her when his breath caught.

"Bo—"

"Clarissa." He stilled her hips with his hand. Tabitha batted at his hand, but he remained firm, not letting her move against him. "Don't move, sweetheart, or I might prove myself wrong and rush this intimacy thing a bit."

"I don't care," she heard herself say shamelessly as a deep, insatiable need drove her. "I want . . ." Oh Lord, she wanted her first orgasm. "You know what I want."

He settled her closer against him and cupped her face. "I told you, *this* is what intimacy is about. Being comfortable together—"

"Bo." She'd made her decision, couldn't he see that? "Kiss me again. Kiss me again and don't stop."

A low laugh, rough with its vibrating intensity, escaped him. He was wearing his easygoing expression, but there behind it, there in the moonlit room, she saw what she wanted—stark need, desire, even fear—which was everything she was feeling. She couldn't possibly resist.

"Hurry, Bo."

His lips brushed her cheek, but she turned quickly, needing to put her mouth to his. In her eagerness, she crashed into his nose, then jerked away feeling hopelessly awkward. He just whispered her name then found her lips with his once sweetly, then again. And again.

She sighed with relief and pleasure because he tasted so good, just as he smelled, and she thought

she could close her eyes and die right then because life couldn't get any better. Then he pressed
her body against his and she nearly *did* die.

His tongue swept over hers and she stopped
thinking. Her self-protected, neglected senses
burst to life, shoving back everything but him,
this. Whispering his name, she tried to put everything she was feeling in her motions as she pulled
him close. "Show me the rest," she begged
against his mouth. "I want you to show me the
rest."

"Clarissa." His voice was low, tight, unbearably husky. "Wait, I—"

"Please." She dragged his head back to hers.
"Please, Bo. I want to feel, I want to be loved. I
want it to be you."

He groaned, then plundered her mouth, rav-
ishing it with his lips, his tongue, his teeth, making her nearly delirious with pleasure.

"More." She clung to him, her hands running
restlessly over his arms, his chest, pulling him
closer and closer. She yanked at his T-shirt, trying to drag it over his head, laughing in relief
when he helped her. "Oh, Bo," she whispered
when she caught sight of his magnificent torso in
the moonlit room. He was broad and hard and
bronzed and gorgeous, and she wanted to touch
him. When her fingers brushed over his skin, she
felt his jolt, the burst of heat and need that exploded from him. She heard him struggle to con-

trol his breathing and instead of terrifying her, it made her drunk with power. "More."

She couldn't believe it was *her* voice she was hearing; begging, demanding, she couldn't believe the overwhelming need. Rearing up, she tugged her blouse out of her pants, then nearly ripped the buttons out of the holes in her haste to feel flesh against flesh.

His fingers came up and brushed hers aside as his mouth raced over her face, her throat, then her neck, and when he'd tugged the silk aside, he dipped his head and tasted her.

Clarissa turned into a bundle of nerve endings as each touch banished any lingering traces of her past. Every inch of her came vibrantly alive; gone was the shame or discomfort she associated with intimacy. She felt such freedom, such control, and oh how she needed more of whatever he was doing to her. "Bo . . ." Her breath caught when he kissed his way over her collarbone to the edge of her lace bra. "Now. I can't stand any more.'

His low, shivery voice was filled with love and laughter. "We haven't even started."

"But . . . oh!" She inhaled and let it out in a shuddery sigh when he gently cupped her breast, skimming over her nipple with a thumb. "I'm ready. *Now.*"

"Are you?" he murmured, never stopping what he was doing to her with his mouth and fingers. Slowly, he pulled the lace aside, lifted his head, and ran his tongue over the tight aching tip.

She clutched at him, an insistent, hungry heat spiraling through her, pooling between her thighs, making her dizzy with desire, moaning as her hips pushed insistently against his.

"I feel funny," she gasped. "I've never felt like this before."

"Good," came his thick reply, but still he moved with none of her hungry urgency, giving her time to retreat, which she had no intention of doing, not now that her insides were on fire. His hands came up to frame her face.

"I've waited too long to rush this," he claimed, but she was beyond patience, and she grabbed fistfuls of his hair and tugged. He chuckled, then grew serious again as she kissed him, and this time it was no simple meeting of the lips. It was deep, wet, and long, and by the time he broke for some desperately needed air, they were both breathless.

No longer certain he could wait, Bo skimmed off her blouse, his gaze glued to the feast of warm curves and flesh he exposed. He unhooked her bra and drew it down her shoulders before he realized Clarissa was holding her breath with her eyes squeezed shut.

"Hey," he whispered, drawing her down on him and banding his arms loosely around her. He had to grit his teeth against the heavenly feel of her bare skin against his. "Clarissa, sweetheart, do you want to stop?"

"No." She opened her eyes but kept her gaze

averted. "I'm—this is—" A loud sigh escaped from her as she dropped her forehead to his chest, hunching her shoulders in defeat. "I've never had an orgasm before," she blurted out miserably. "I don't know if I can. It never mattered before because I didn't really like the whole thing anyway, but with you it's different, I like it a lot, and oh, God. I'm so embarrassed. Bo, what if I fail?"

He swallowed hard as his heart overfilled. Cupping her face, he tipped it back up to his. "It's not a test. Besides, if anyone is going to fail here, it's going to be me."

That made her look at him. "Why?"

"Because I haven't . . . done this in over five years. To be honest, I'm not even sure if I can."

"You said you could."

"I can achieve orgasm," he assured her, already more than halfway there from just touching her. "But without my legs I'm not sure how well I can actually . . . perform."

A light came into her eyes then, a challenging, excited light. "I bet you can," she whispered. "If I help."

"Yeah?" Whatever blood had been left in his head drained rapidly, leaving rational thought difficult. "Well, I bet you can, too, if *I* help." Their smiles faded as they dove at each other, kissing, touching, moaning, and grasping at their remaining clothing. He tugged at her pants, helping her as she reared up to slide them off. She had to sit up to pull down his sweats, which gave Bo a bad moment. He hated the way his legs looked, all thin and useless and pathetic, but Clarissa, beautiful in her newly discovered power of desire, never hesitated.

Kneeling nude over him, her pale skin shimmering in the faint light, she looked at him expectantly.

And for a moment regret overshadowed his rage of passion. "I wish I could pick you up. I want to carry you to my bed—"

"No, Bo," came her quick, soft reply. "It doesn't matter. There's nowhere else I want to be."

"But—"

She sat on him, which pretty much shut him up.

"Come here," he demanded, tugging her down. "Come here and let me love you." Gently spreading her thighs wider over him, he brought her face to his for a kiss. "I want to watch you lose yourself," he said against her lips. "I want to watch you when you come for the first time and know it was for me." His fingers slipped down over her belly to touch her, drawing a finger slowly and knowingly over her needy center, closing his eyes when she gasped and clutched him tighter. Her nails dug in deeper and so did his finger, sinking into her as his thumb kept up the light torture on her throbbing center. Above him, looking like a goddess, Clarissa threw back her head, her breath sobbing out in shocky pants as her hips rocked against his. "Please," she whispered. "Don't stop. Don't ever stop."

"I won't," he promised. Craving drove him, a craving to see her explode in ecstasy over him, to see her lost in the heat and abandon he knew she'd never experienced before. Then she gasped as she bucked and stiffened, then bucked again.

He caught her as she collapsed over his body, quivering and trembling and damp with perspiration, breath heaving as if she'd run a marathon. "I never knew . . . I never imagined," she murmured shakily into his chest a moment later.

He tried to respond, but his body was hard and hot, and so damned needy he thought he might break down and cry if she didn't take him now.

Lifting her head, she bit her lip. "Would it be greedy here to ask for more?"

"God, no." And he helped her straddle him again. She reached down, her fist closing around him, gliding and stroking. His vision faded. "Wait," he managed to grate out, gripping her hips. His body pulsed and leaped and was so close to its goal, he broke out into a sweat. "Clarissa, sweetheart, I'm not protected. Hell, I'm not even prepared."

She blinked at him innocently, then understanding dawned. "Oh . . . Are you safe?"

"Five years' worth," he vowed with a tense laugh.

"I'm safe too." She bit her lip, gazed down at

his chest, suddenly shy. "I . . . can't get preg-nant, Bo."

She couldn't get pregnant. The words entered his fuzzy, desire-muddled brain, so did the soul-deep sadness of Clarissa's tone, but he couldn't stop for explanations. Not now, not with her sweet, delectable, bare body poised over him, ready, willing, and able.

"Bo?" she whispered, emotion clogging her voice.

"It's okay, sweetheart. Then there's nothing stopping us." He tugged her down for a drugging kiss, his fingers dipping down, but she was still hot, still ready. Watching her face, he eased into her, so slowly, he thought he might die of joy and hunger before he was all the way in.

But she took every inch of him, and he was never more thankful for the nightly workouts that had kept his stomach, hip, and thigh muscles strong and supple. She clung to him, her head thrown back in wild abandon. Her body glowed and he couldn't help but pull her down to taste whatever he could reach; her throat, her shoulder, her breasts. She moved, too, hesitantly at first, then, with his urging hands on her hips, she gained confidence, until her hips rocked and rocked and he was groaning and calling out her name hoarsely.

He kissed her again, angling her pistoning hips so he could thrust deeper, then deeper still. Beyond all reason, he buried his face in her throat. He felt her climax again, felt her soft tremors as she cried out and was lost in that dark pleasure. He couldn't hold back another second, not even for her, and even as he thought it, the wave took him, and he shuddered as he gave himself up to the pure, blinding, enveloping bliss.

Clarissa sighed against him, a long, very satisfied sigh that made him smile. He could lie like this, his face pressed against her skin, stroking her damp, hot back forever. A lump filled his throat at the thought, making it difficult to speak. He never imagined he could feel like this ever again, so whole and alive and happy. How he wanted to believe it could last, but he knew better.

"Oh, Bo." She hugged him with a death grip, laughing and crying at the same time. "I feel so . . . normal."

He couldn't catch his breath; she looked so beautiful, so powerful. *So his.*

She lifted her head and smiled at him in the dim light. "I think I want to do that again."

He couldn't keep his body from leaping to instant attention at her hesitant tone, couldn't stop his hips from thrusting helplessly upward.

Her eyes lit up as she felt his reaction. "Oh . . ."

He started to laugh, but it died in his throat when she kissed him. As she did she let her hands roam over the planes of his chest, molding her fingers to the contours of muscle, her silky hair brushing over his body, his hips, his belly.

"Can we?" She whispered.

As if he could refuse that eager, beautiful voice anything, especially this. "Oh yeah, again . . . and again," he whispered, and tugged her closer to make good on his promise.

THIRTEEN

Clarissa came awake in slow degrees, with the sun blaring in the windows.

Stretching in Bo's huge bed, which they'd worked their way to sometime in the predawn hours, she found the sheets cold.

When had he left?

Flipping onto her back, she stared at the ceiling and grinned at her memories of the night, going back and reliving each and every one of them. Slowly her grin faded into a frown. Why had he left?

Leaping to her feet, she whirled around, trying to remember just where she'd left her clothes.

Scattered across Bo's living room. Blushing a little, she reached for what looked like a discarded T-shirt. As she slipped it over her head she inhaled Bo's scent and closed her eyes.

A minute later she entered the kitchen and

found him sitting by a garden window, staring out at the morning, a mug of steaming coffee in his hands.

"Morning," he said, his hot, searching gaze running over *his* shirt on her body.

When had the sound of his voice begun to mean so much? When had his mahogany eyes, filled with such an intriguing mixture of affection and hunger, and something she couldn't quite name, started to draw her so? "Hi," she said inanely.

He'd showered, and changed into clean jeans and a polo shirt, clearly ready for work. But something about this morning was different from anything she'd seen on him before.

Though he sat in his chair, a set of braces covered his legs. And suddenly she recognized that emotion in his gaze for what it was—nervousness—and her own nerve endings started dancing. God, she was an idiot, for she had seen him in braces, once before, the night he'd fallen in the gym. Only then her concern had been his health and it hadn't sunk in. Until now.

He avoided her eyes as he spoke again. "I left you some hot water in the shower if you'd like."

Because her tongue refused to work, she could only nod. *Why* were his legs in braces? Only one reason she could think of. As she started to move back out of the room, feeling a little dense and awkward, he set down his mug and moved in his chair fluidly toward her, grabbing her hand to bring her to a halt.

"Clarissa, about last night."

Her heart plummeted as she looked down at him. She'd just discovered her feelings for him, and he'd lost interest and no longer wanted her. Maybe during the night he'd learned she was nothing but a bed hog, a pillow and blanket stealer, and he needed a more considerate woman—

"I can't stop thinking about your life before," he whispered. "I can't stop picturing you being treated so cruelly." His voice was rough and gritty, his eyes suspiciously bright. "How do you bear it?"

"Bad things happen to people." She touched his chair, keeping her eyes off the steel and leather covering his legs. "You know that better than most."

"I don't want bad things to happen to *you*. Not ever again."

"If there's one thing I've learned, it's that you can't always protect people from getting hurt."

His eyes hardened. "I might be in a wheelchair at this moment, but I can still raise hell, believe me. If your father ever gets out of prison—"

"Bo, no." Fear for him clenched her heart. "*No.* That part of my life is long over."

"Then why are you so afraid of your brother and what he wants to tell you?"

"Because I'm silly. I'm allowing my childhood fears to get the best of me, and I'm not going to do it anymore. I'm tougher than that."

"And you're not alone." His eyes softened as they caressed her. "Last night was incredible, Clarissa. I never dreamed it could be so good for me ever again."

"I didn't think it could ever be that good *period.*" She felt the blush redden her cheeks as she remembered some of the things they'd done, how he'd made her feel as if she were the only woman on earth. In one night, he'd given her back her confidence in herself as a woman, all while teaching and showing her how love should be.

A shiver of anticipation ran through her. She wondered what he'd say if she told him she'd decided the hell with her fears, she was ready to try trust. Love. While her body rejoiced at the thought, her mind had no idea how to utter the words. "Bo, I know I told you I wanted to be just friends, but what I felt for you last night wasn't just friendly."

His hand dropped hers. His eyes darkened. With a quick, jerky motion, he spun away from her.

She followed him to the set of windows that looked down on the rough, turbulent ocean. "Somehow," she said with a lightness she didn't feel, "I thought that might be met with more enthusiasm."

He didn't respond.

"What's the matter?"

"This, for one." He gestured to his legs.

"You're not going to let a little thing like your chair come between us, are you?" she quipped nervously.

Carefully, he backed away from her, as if he didn't trust himself to remain too close. "This chair *is* between us. In case you haven't noticed, it dictates my every move."

"Well, so does what happened to me, but I'm not going to let it anymore."

"This is different," he argued. "You can't compare this chair with what happened to you."

"Why not? We were both victims." She smiled, nerves and fear and hope mingling. "Let's get over it together, Bo."

"I *am* over it," he said, fisting his hands on his thighs. "Dammit, I am. And though I am going to kick myself later for saying this, you deciding you want me isn't enough."

"Why?"

"Without this chair, you'd have never looked twice at me." His tone was harsh, rough with emotion. "Do you have any idea how that makes me feel?"

"Special?" she asked hopefully, but he only snorted and shook his head. She dropped the desperate joking and sank to her knees before him, grabbing his hands. "Oh, Bo. I can't be too late to decide I've been a fool."

He swallowed hard. "Don't blame yourself.

It's more than that." He looked out into the morning sun. "You've been honest with me and I have to be honest back." Gently, he pushed her away and rolled back to the window, picking up what looked like a set of banded steel poles. With a flick of his wrist, it expanded into a walker.

He shot her an indecipherable glance, then scooted forward on his chair. Awkwardly, with several grunts and a pithy oath, he pulled himself to his feet. Leaning heavily on the walker, he looked into her eyes, his both bleak and triumphant.

"You're standing." Granted, he looked like a light wind could knock him over, but he stood there on his own two wavering feet, tall and undeniably proud.

"Yes."

"Oh, my God." She felt a little sick, even as a laugh bubbled. Her eyes filled. "Oh, my God."

"That night you found me in the gym, when I'd fallen . . ." He inhaled sharply and hesitated a moment. "I'd been practicing walking. With my braces." Gripping the walker, he shoved it in front of him. He tightened his jaw and pulled one leg at a time forward.

He stopped and looked at her from beneath his lashes. "I know it looks pretty pathetic—"

"No," she burst out, blinking back the welling tears. But as she spoke, she stepped back. "It's amazing. But you said you couldn't."

"I still can't do it without the damn braces and

this stupid walker. I probably never will. And it's so slow it drives me crazy."

"That's why you use the chair?"

"That, and if I keep these braces on too long, I get agonizing cramps that lay me up pretty good." He looked grim. "But I'll keep trying. If I keep working out—"

"Torturing yourself, you mean," she grated.

His eyes flashed. "You're not upset at *me*, Clarissa. Don't you dare try to make me believe that. You're mad at yourself because the sight of me standing like this makes you sick to your stomach. No, dammit, don't deny it. You're turning green already."

"I'm not."

"You're mad because you've changed your mind. You don't want me anymore, not now that you know I can do this."

She needed to sit down because her knees were trembling. But Bo seemed so big, so tall, so unexpectedly huge . . . suddenly she couldn't sit, not when he would tower over her. Stumbling back a bit, she leaned into the windowsill and concentrated on breathing.

"I can't hide this," he said hoarsely, everything he felt in his eyes as he watched her suffer. "I love you, Clarissa. But I can't hide this, not even for you."

"Oh, my God," she repeated. The tears fell unbidden because she was utterly incapable of hiding them as her world rocked on its axis. "You *love* me."

A bittersweet smile crossed his face. He lifted a shoulder, started to nod, then nearly toppled to the floor. She leaped to him with a small cry, throwing her arms around his waist to catch him.

He dropped the walker and held on tight to her. "I do love you, Clarissa. Please, can't you find it in your heart to let go of the past? To love me back, just the way I am?"

Could she?

With all her newly found heart, she tried to say the words he wanted to hear. But she looked at him, felt him hard and sure against her, and fumbled.

"I don't know," she whispered. "I'm sorry, I just don't know."

His hands rose up to gently touch her shoulders, to push her away from his rigid body. He sank back into his chair.

His face, normally tanned and happy, looked pale and miserable. "I never pegged you for a quitter."

She felt frozen, stiff with shock, and hated herself for that. "I don't know what to say to you."

"How about, 'drive me home, please, since I'm going to give up the love of a lifetime because I'm dumb.' "

She crossed her arms over her chest. "Oh, that was mature."

"Mature?" He choked on the word. "You want *mature?* Fine." He schooled his face into an expression of blankness. "Take your time, Clarissa. You have the rest of your life to waste."

She refused to be baited. "What does your doctor say about you walking?"

A shadow crossed his face as he made himself comfortable in the chair. Wincing, he used his hands to straighten out his leg, and she suspected he was feeling some of those agonizing cramps he'd talked about. "You know how they are. All doom and gloom."

"Bo." It was beginning to occur to her that maybe he hadn't quite adjusted to his new life as much as she thought he had.

"What does it matter what he says? Only I can control my body." But his own doubt was obvious. "And I will control it."

"It's okay if you never do," she said softly, alarmed at how adamant he seemed. What disappointment had he set himself up for?

"You wish."

Stung, she stared at him. "How can you say that?"

"All right." He straightened his shoulders and glared at her. "Tell me it's not true. Tell me that *when* I walk, you'll feel the same way about me that you did last night—that you did this morning before you saw me stand up!"

She crossed her arms over her chest and glared right back, not even realizing she was facing him down without fear of repercussions. "All I asked is what your doctor said."

"It doesn't matter." He ran a hand down his legs and grimaced. "I won't give up, Clarissa. Now do you see the problem? I won't give up and you won't give in."

She'd awakened this morning thinking herself in love with a tender, passionate man who would give her the world. That world had turned upside down, leaving her staring at a tall, powerfully built man more than capable of turning his clear temper on her.

Bo watched her, his expression going darker and bleaker by the moment. "I can see the idea of me out of this chair just thrills the hell out of you."

The cruelty of the whole thing tore at her. She was wrong, and she knew it, but she couldn't get past the images her mind had locked on, images of Bo, formidable and angry.

Unnerved, she backed away from him, her thoughts whirling.

Would it matter if he never sat in his chair again? If he walked? She'd like to think not, but her heart wouldn't slow down, telling her the sorry truth.

She just didn't know.

FOURTEEN

"Married yet?"

Bo groaned at his baby sister Laurie's voice and closed his eyes. Shoving away stacks of paperwork he'd been trying to occupy his mind with, he leaned his elbows on his desk and sighed. "If I said yes, will you go away?"

Light laughter filled the phone line. "Mom made me call. Kim told her you sounded depressed, so now Mom's got everyone in the family lined up to call you over the next few days."

"Terrific."

"You're not, are you?" Laurie's voice sobered, and though she was only three years younger than Bo, she sounded like a worried kid. "Depressed, I mean."

"No, Laurie." He remembered those first few horrible months after his accident, when he'd felt as though a big black cloud had sucked out all his emotions. It had hung over his head, so that he could hardly see or hear, and hadn't cared that he couldn't. It'd terrified everyone in the family, and he knew they still feared for him. "I'm fine."

"You have been kind of quiet the past few weeks."

Had it only been a few weeks? he wondered. It seemed Clarissa Woods had been stirring up his life much longer than that. Then he remembered how she'd looked wearing nothing but his T-shirt over her willowy body and he got stirred up all over again.

"Bo, I have a friend I want you to meet, and—"

"Jeez, not you too." He pinched the bridge of his nose and struggled to not lose his patience. "You've been married only six months, Laurie. *Six months*. Stop worrying about me and go do whatever it is married couples do."

"Can't. Already had sex this morning."

He groaned. "Stop. I absolutely don't want to hear this."

She giggled. "Twice."

"Laurie!"

"Now, Bo." She trailed out his name until it sounded like a song. "Mom's worried and you know how she is when she gets upset over one of her own. She's rallied all of us together, determined we fix your life."

He should have stayed in bed, he realized. In bed with Clarissa sleeping peacefully in his arms.

Maybe if he hadn't gotten up, if he hadn't left her alone to awaken, maybe things wouldn't have gotten so out of control.

"My life doesn't need fixing," he told his sister, which he knew was a bold-faced lie. It *did* need fixing, and quick, or he would lose the only woman who'd ever meant anything to him.

"Tell Mom—" he snapped, only to stop abruptly, letting his breath out slowly. He closed his eyes. God, he was going to blow up at Laurie and it wasn't her fault. She didn't deserve it; she loved him and was worried.

How was he to tell her his frustration had absolutely nothing to do with her? That it came from remembering the look on Clarissa's face as he stood on his own two feet? Realizing how little headway he'd made with her, how little she really trusted him, had nearly killed him. "I'm sorry, Laurie . . . I'm just tired."

"No, that's more than *tired* talking," Laurie said with certainty. "What's the matter, Bo?"

"Nothing." He tossed off his melancholy and forced a smile into his voice. "Tell Mom I'm working on that wife for her, okay?"

"You are?" she squeaked in surprise. "But you've always said you'd never marry."

It was true, and he had no idea when exactly that had changed. But he wanted a wife now, and he wanted that wife to be Clarissa. He had no idea how things had gotten so screwed up, how they'd managed to alienate each other so badly when all he wanted to do was love her for the rest of his life.

God, he'd been so proud of his efforts with the braces, so sure she trusted him enough to be just as proud.

How wrong he'd been.

"Bo, is there something you're not telling us?" Laurie demanded, sounding excited. "Are you going to elope or something?"

"No eloping," he promised. "And no, there's nothing to tell you." He thought of life without Clarissa and felt his heart darken. They simply had to work it out. "Yet."

"Bo!"

"Bye, Laurie."

When he hung up, he lifted his head and discovered Jeff and Sheila standing in his doorway with wide, stupid grins on their faces. And though Sheila had at least four inches on Jeff, he had an arm wrapped loosely around her waist, looking like a lovestruck fool.

A bolt of jealousy streaked hot through him, but at their obvious delight with each other, he bit it back. It wasn't too tough since he'd loved them both forever. "Hey, guys." He managed a grin at Sheila. "Looks like you got lucky last night."

Sheila laughed. "Yep. Couple of times."

Jeff, looking quite proud of himself, grinned from ear to ear. They were so lucky, Bo thought. So lucky to have found each other.

He'd known love all his life; his family had

made sure of it. But *nothing* compared with how he felt for Clarissa. He couldn't believe how stupid he'd been.

Of course it was easy for him to accept how he felt for her. Even after what had happened to him, he'd never doubted himself or his worth. Because of all the love and affection that had always been showered on him, he'd never wondered if someone could indeed love him. He'd always taken it for granted.

But Clarissa had never had *anyone* unconditionally love her, had never been showered with affection and easy emotion the way he had.

Jeff smiled at him. "I'm on my way in to work with Michael. Want to come play some ball with him?"

"Sure."

Bo watched as Sheila gave Jeff a quick hug and kiss, promise heavy in her eyes, as she left to go back to her station. In that moment Bo would have given anything for Clarissa to come in with love shining in her eyes, to have her launch herself at *him* with a hug and kiss.

Hell, he'd settle for a smile.

Instead, she'd arrived at work one minute before her shift, only to don her coat and quickly disappear into her first patient's room without a word.

No smile, and certainly no kiss and hug.

She hadn't even looked at him.

His gut clenched.

"Bo?"

He looked at Jeff. "Yeah. I'm coming."

He wheeled to the gym, counting on the small, brave boy to lift his spirits. It didn't take long.

Michael tired quickly, so Bo set the little guy on his lap while he and Jeff went one-on-one. Michael gripped Bo's neck with his one arm, while Bo used one hand to steer and one to dribble. Occasionally, when Michael got too excited and let go, Bo had to drop the ball to catch and hold the laughing, squirming boy. He never minded.

Even *with* Michael to hold on to, he won the first round by four points. Gasping, Jeff slid down the wall and sat.

He shook his head in disgust. "I can't believe how bad I am."

"Nah." Bo grinned, panting and sweating. "I'm just good."

Michael stared up at him with adoration in his eyes. "I want to be as good as you."

Bo leaned his head back as he tried to catch his breath, and decided exercise was good for the soul, because holding a contented Michael and having just kicked Jeff's butt on the court allowed him a precious few moments of peace.

Until he remembered Clarissa, and the pain in her eyes as she'd backed away from the sight of him in leg braces. He glanced at Michael, who was holding the ball reverently.

"That's it," Bo encouraged when Michael ran

his one hand over the basketball. He was far too small and weak to actually dribble, though they were working on that.

"Feel it," Bo encouraged. "Soon you'll be able to bounce it alongside your chair like I do."

"Just what I need," Jeff muttered, but grinned. "I'll have two of you to lose to."

"When?" Michael asked eagerly. "When will I be that good?"

Secretly Bo thought it might be a while. Michael had let his arm atrophy badly, and he also had to work on his chest muscles. Besides that, he was only five. But the light of hope sparkling in his eyes was too much to resist. "Soon. Real soon."

"It's my wish," Michael confided, cuddling closer. "You know, when you go to bed every night and make a wish on a falling star?"

Bo nodded with a sad smile, and overcome by sudden emotion, he rubbed his cheek over the boy's head. If Bo went to bed tonight and made his wish, what would happen?

"I wish to play basketball. For real." Michael looked at Bo with an open smile. "Clarissa said God answered all wishes, but sometimes not the way we want."

A lump the size of a regulation basketball formed in Bo's throat and he held Michael close, unable to speak.

"Women are pretty smart," Jeff said.

Michael nodded against Bo's chest as he

stroked the ball with his one arm. "She told me her dream."

"Did she?"

The boy beamed at Bo, his heart in his eyes. "She said her dream was that *you* got your wish. What's your wish, Bo?"

Bo was sure he'd fall apart right then and there, but he smiled through it. "It's sort of complicated."

"What's so com-caked about wanting to walk again?"

Bo stared at the boy, then let out a little laugh. God. Of course Michael thought Bo's wish would be to walk. Clarissa believed it as well. Hell, up until last night, if anyone had asked Bo himself what his greatest wish was, he'd have announced the same.

But he would have been wrong.

He did indeed have a wish, and it had nothing to do with his legs.

He wished for Clarissa.

Clarissa arrived at her condo after work that night to find her brother, Sean, sitting on her steps.

Her heart stopped, and for a second she wished she'd taken Bo up on his offer to drive her home. Not that she and Bo had exchanged more than three words all day, and those had been very awkward words at that, but when she'd gone into the kitchen to get her purse, he'd been waiting with the offer.

Unable to face him after all that they'd said to each other that morning, she'd politely turned him down, his obvious pain mingling with hers.

But now she wished for him to be by her side.

"Hey, sis," Sean said. He stood, tall and looking so like her father, she nearly stepped back. "I know how you feel about your privacy, and I would never have breached it, but this is important—"

"How did you find me?" Clarissa demanded, fear welling. Good Lord, if *he* found her, then so could her father.

"It wasn't easy, believe me." He didn't make a move to hold out a hand or hug her. He wouldn't, for despite their blood ties and upbringing, they'd never once shared physical affection. Never a hug, a kiss, or even a touch.

Just another legacy from their childhood.

But now, after being in California for only a matter of weeks, things had changed for Clarissa.

For the first time in her life she would have welcomed a kiss from Sean. A hug even, or just a simple touch. Some sign that they were indeed flesh and blood, that he recognized their relationship, and that he loved her.

"Are you all right?" he asked.

His concern sank in and she knew she had to accept that in lieu of physical affection. He didn't mean to hurt her, he just didn't know any better than she did how to show love. "I'm fine."

"You should have called me back, Clarissa." He stared at her with blue eyes that matched her own. Eyes well trained to hide all emotions.

"Why? So you could tell me that Robert"—she never thought of her father as "Dad"—"is out of jail? I'd rather not know."

Sean paled. "You don't understand."

Her stomach clenched and her legs went so weak, she plopped down on the step. "Oh, God. It's true?"

"Yeah, but not in the way you think," Sean said, his voice unrecognizable as it cracked. He hunkered down in front of her and for the first time in his entire life he let her see what he was thinking. Pain clouded his eyes as his face crumpled in shock and grief. "He had a heart attack. He's dead."

Clarissa accompanied Sean to Texas that night, her mind blank with shock. She would have liked to bury herself in her painting and be alone to think, but Sean had looked so young, so lost, she hadn't been able to leave him alone to make the arrangements.

She'd called in and left a message for Sheila at The Right Place, saying she was horribly sorry but she needed five days off starting immediately.

She'd tried to call Bo, had lifted the phone and

dialed his number at least a dozen times, only to set the phone back down before she'd connected.

What would she say?

That night, for the first time since he'd gotten out of the hospital after his accident, Bo skipped his workout. Suddenly, or maybe not so suddenly, there was something far more important than his mobility.

Clarissa.

He drove directly to her condo, charged with emotion, champing at the bit, unable to wait to tell her what he'd discovered. That he loved her with all his heart and soul. That he wanted to give her as much time as she needed to get used to the idea of loving him back, because he wouldn't give up proving she could trust him.

But to his great disappointment, she wasn't home. With no choice left but to drive home, he wished he'd never waited so long to figure it all out, wished he didn't have to sleep without her safe in his arms.

After a sleepless night during which he must have tried calling Clarissa a hundred times, Bo drove like a maniac into work, desperate for a glimpse of her. Needing to prove to himself that he hadn't scared her off for good.

Sheila came to his office immediately, looking

pale and grim. She never looked this way, *never*, and fear gripped him.

"What is it?"

"Oh, honey. I'm so sorry," she said.

"Why?"

"Because you got your heart broken and I think it's my fault."

"Oh, please," he muttered. "Not you too. I've got enough meddling females in my life." He rolled past her and moved to his desk. "Is Clarissa in yet?"

"Tell me what happened, Bo. Tell me and you'll feel better." She maneuvered into his office and, shoving aside her walker, sank into a chair, waiting.

"What is this?" he demanded, frustration from a sleepless night stirring his temper. "You and Jeff get together and now everyone else has to have a happy ending as well?"

Her patience never dimmed as she smiled at him sadly, concern for him flowing from her caring eyes. "What happened with her, Bo?"

"Nothing. Everything."

"Oh, honey, I never thought she'd hurt you. I'm so sorry."

"It was sort of a mutual hurting, Sheila. And I think most of it might have been my fault."

"It takes two," she said firmly, loyal in her friendship.

"Not in this case."

"Don't blame yourself."

"Well, at the moment, I can't think of anyone else *to* blame." He slammed a fist down on his desk. "Dammit. Where is she?"

Sheila met his gaze with difficulty. "She's gone. She left a message that she'll be away for five days."

"Gone?"

"Can't you tell me what happened?"

He couldn't take her sympathy. "What happened is I was an idiot and pushed her when I had no business pushing her. *There.* Are you satisfied? I spilled my guts, admitted I love her. I can't live without her, and now she's gone!" By the time he got to the last sentence, he was shouting.

Without a word, Sheila grabbed her walker and got up, slowly making her way toward him.

He shook his head sharply, but ignoring him, she pushed his chair around so she could envelop him in her arms.

"I'm so sorry," she whispered, with far more compassion than Bo thought he could take. "She'll be back," she promised, hugging him tight, but even Bo could hear the doubt in her voice. "She'll be back."

"Yeah."

FIFTEEN

Clarissa and Sean buried their father two days later. Pathetically few people came to his service, but Clarissa didn't care.

She just wanted the whole thing to be over.

On the third day, she went to her father's gravesite. Alone except for miles of grass and thousands of headstones, she lay back and studied the lazy, endless Texas sky.

All her feelings and emotions had been in a deep freeze for the past few days. She hadn't allowed any thoughts to crowd her mind except about what needed to be done. Now, with nothing left to do, she started to defrost.

And it hurt.

Not about her father. She'd be a hypocrite if she truly grieved for him. Oh, she had some feelings of regret for a wasted life, sadness for a childhood that would never be, but that was it.

He was gone, and just that simply, the wicked witch of her life was dead.

She had nothing left to tie her to her past. No reason at all not to leap back into the life she'd created for herself. In fact, she had a new lease on it.

Never again would she have to be afraid.

But she was, for she'd cultivated her fear and hate and shame, hugged it close because it helped her to remember not to trust, that love always hurt.

But she'd been wrong because she *could* trust, she could love, be loved in return. How foolish she'd been. It wasn't Bo walking that had so terrified her. She knew he'd never hurt her.

It had been her own fear of letting go, and she'd blamed him. Blamed the man she'd fallen in love with.

Oh, how she wanted him. *Now.* And the truth was, she wanted him no matter if he sat, stood, walked, or raced marathons. Whole and healthy or sick and hurting—with or without legs—she wanted Bo.

She wanted him more than her own life, and had no idea how to prove it to him.

Closing her eyes, she forced herself to concentrate. And slowly an idea formed.

With her face to the sun, her whole life ahead of her, she smiled. She'd used only three of the five days she'd told Sheila she needed, so she had two days left in which to put that idea to good use.

If she hurried, she could do it.

Five torturously long days after Clarissa left, Bo saw the last patient and employee out of The Right Place and made his way to the gym. His workouts had lost much of their intensity over the past few nights, and he knew that while he would continue to exercise, he'd never again push himself to exhaustion or to the point of being sick.

Without Clarissa it wasn't worth it.

Pulling himself out of his chair and onto a bench, he started the long, tedious process of strapping on the leg braces. It took him long minutes to walk/drag himself with the walker over to a set of parallel bars.

He'd just made it, and was huffing and puffing, leaning on the bars, when he heard the door open behind him.

He froze, bracing himself for the familiar sense of humiliation to hit him. For five years he'd hated this, the feeling of being vulnerable and exposed. Hated even more having his private workout interrupted. But when his mind shifted, he realized he didn't feel shame at all over how his legs looked, or that someone was seeing him trying to better himself.

He felt pride.

Seemed he'd been a fool in more ways than one.

Glancing up in the mirror, he received his second shock.

Clarissa stood there, wearing a soft-looking floral dress he'd never seen before. Its scoop-necked bodice clung to her slender torso, the skirt flaring at her hips to fall around her calves. Her usually braided hair lay in waves past her shoulders, framing her face. Her lips curved in an unsure smile, as if she had no idea what sort of welcome she would receive.

"Clarissa." His voice sounded husky, rough with relief, but he couldn't have hidden his emotions, even if he'd wanted to.

Biting her lip, she resettled a large, wrapped package she held and shut the door behind her. "Hello, Bo." Her blue eyes were shining with both apprehension and joy. "Are you busy?"

He let out a frustrated half growl, half laugh. "Busy going insane about you."

"I—oh." She looked down at the package, then, as if she'd made a monumental decision about something, she lifted her chin with resolve. "I have something for you. I hope I'm not too late." Without waiting for his reaction, she bent, and all that glorious hair fell, covering her face, hiding her expression, so he could only guess at the meaning of her sudden reappearance in his life.

He heard paper ripping, and before he could

decide whether to kiss her or yell at her, she straightened, holding the most gorgeous painting of a seascape he'd ever seen. The sky stretched wide and clear and blue over a sea as deep as forever. On the shore, before a bluff of sand and wild brush, sat a well-tended cottage, its door open in welcome. He could almost smell the salt air, feel the cool breeze on his face, and he marveled at the talent used to create it.

Then he recognized that painting as the one he'd seen in unfinished form at Clarissa's apartment all those weeks ago, and felt overwhelmed by the gift she was offering him.

Swallowing hard, she gave him another shaky smile. "I hope you like it."

"I thought you didn't want to share your art," he managed to say around the huge lump in his throat.

She seemed to have difficulty speaking as well, though her gaze never left his. In her eyes he saw his heart, his soul, and hers in return. "I was wrong," she admitted quietly. She licked her lips, looking nervous. "I want you to have it, Bo. I painted it for you."

Words failed him.

"I'm glad I found you in here tonight," she went on. "I don't think I could have waited until tomorrow to see you."

"I wish I'd have found you days ago." Because he felt shakier than usual, and he knew he was about to collapse to the floor, he grabbed the walker. Awkwardly, he dragged his way the few steps to the closest bench, where he sank gratefully. "I've been going crazy, Clarissa."

Regret filled those eyes now, but still, she didn't come any closer, still looking unsure of her welcome. He ended that immediately by raising a hand and lifting it toward her. "Come here."

"I didn't mean to hurt you," she said, not moving. "I said things to you, things that make me cringe now. . . ." Purposely she looked at his legs, at the braces that covered them. "I want you as whole and healthy as I plan on being. And if you can walk without getting hurt, then I want that as well."

Hope sang through his veins, but he had a confession to make too. Had to tell her that his obsession with his walking had taken a backseat to her. "Clarissa—"

"Please," she begged softly, clasping her hands. "I have to say this." She drew a deep breath, then let it out slowly. "I was looking at it all wrong. *You're* not the handicapped one, Bo, *I* am. *Was*." Her smile trembled. "I don't want you to ever give up trying to walk, and I mean that with all my heart." She still didn't move. "My father died."

Another shock, but Bo absorbed it as he looked at her, gauging her emotions. No grief, which he was glad about, because he wouldn't have wanted her to waste any on the bastard, but still . . . there were faint purple smudges beneath her lovely eyes, giving her a weary, exhausted-to-the-bone look that worried him. "Please, sweetheart. Come here."

At the endearment, her eyes filled. Slowly she moved toward his outstretched arms. "I wasn't sure you'd want to see me. The last time we spoke—"

"The last time we spoke we were both feeling a little raw."

Finally she came close enough that he could wrap his arms around her and pull her down next to him. "You feel so good." He buried his face in her hair. "I'm so sorry you went through that alone."

"It doesn't matter."

"It does to me." Unable to get close enough, he tightened his grip, inhaled her sweet, wild scent that never failed to drive him nuts. "You went back to Texas?"

"For the first three and a half days."

"I hate thinking of you alone back there."

"I had Sean."

"I'd like to meet him." And make sure I like him, Bo thought. But finally, the math set in and he pulled back to look into her face. "Where were you for the past day and a half?"

Clearly not ready to handle face-to-face, Clarissa once again buried herself closer, ducking her head beneath his chin. "Painting."

Her face was plastered against his throat, and

the movement of her lips as she spoke gave him a shiver.

As if she felt the same burst of heat, she slid her mouth along the skin of his neck, stopping at the base, where his pulse raced. She kissed him softly.

He squeezed her tighter, closer, wanting never to let her go. "I'm so glad you're here."

"Are you, Bo?" came her low, urgent whisper as her lips and breath fanned his skin. "Are you really?"

"God, yes." He ran his hands over her body to assure himself it was really her. "I rushed you about us, Clarissa, and I'm so sorry for that. I was thinking only about myself, and how you made me feel. It just felt so good, so right for me, I didn't stop to think about how difficult it would be for you to accept *my* feelings, much less *yours*." Rubbing his cheek against her hair, he closed his eyes and vowed, "No matter how impatient I get, I won't push you again. I promise."

Her arms tightened, then loosened so she could lift her head and stare into his face. The fear he'd hoped never to see again leaped in her eyes. "Have you—I mean, you haven't changed your mind about how you feel for me—"

"God no," came his explosive protest. "I—"

"Wait!" Cupping his face in her hands, she met his gaze. How she wanted to close her eyes, but she forced herself to be brave. "I love you, Bo. I meant to tell you first thing, right after I told you what a fool I've been, letting my past rule my life." She sagged a little in his arms as the words escaped, feeling as if a terrible weight had been lifted. "I love you with all my heart."

"Clarissa—"

"Shhh." Blocking the words he wanted so desperately to say with one hand, she used her other to caress his jaw. "There's something I want to do." But she broke off, unsure. For a second that horrible sense of self-consciousness she'd lived with all her life blasted her, but she forced it back.

Gently, but with purpose, she removed her fingers from his lips and covered them with her own. She felt his start of surprise, but she held his face and deepened their connection, swallowing his low murmur of approval. It made her delirious with power to continue the kiss when he would have broken off.

"Clarissa, sweetheart . . . " he gasped when they surfaced for air. "Let me—"

"No, *let me*." Leaning forward, she devoured his mouth again. "I want to seduce you, Bo. I want you to let me."

He let out a choked laugh that ended on a moan when she streaked her hands beneath his T-shirt to touch his bare chest. His heart beat wildly, and feeling his barely contained hunger gave her another surge of power. She could do this. Hell, she could do anything. "Oh, Bo, I love to touch you."

Throwing her arms around his back, she

nipped his ear, which caught him off balance. He wasn't used to her being the aggressive one, she realized with delight, gently biting him again. Wavering wildly on the bench, they both toppled heavily to the floor, with poor Bo on the bottom, taking the brunt of the weight.

Frightened she'd hurt him, Clarissa reared up, an apology on her lips, but Bo merely growled and tugged her back down.

"Where do you think you're going?" he wanted to know as he held her close. "You were busy, remember?"

"Yes." She laughed then groaned as his mouth found her throat. "I was trying to seduce you. Stop that and let me do it." But as she settled her body over him the metal of his leg braces bit into the skin of her thighs and calves.

With an oath, Bo pulled away, clearly humiliated, but she couldn't let him, absolutely *refused* to let him withdraw now. "Strip," she ordered breathlessly, tugging at his T-shirt, determined to sidetrack him. "Now."

A slow, lazy grin replaced the embarrassment, and he obeyed, lifting off the shirt and flinging it across the room. "Bossy little thing, aren't you?"

With love, hope, and joy racing through her veins, she nodded, spreading her palms over his magnificent chest and flat belly. "You're so beautiful, Bo." She leaned forward, planting warm openmouthed kisses near his navel.

Sucking in his breath, Bo leaned forward to

start working on the long line of buttons that ran down her dress. His shaking fingers had only opened the first few, and he'd just gotten a tantalizing peek at creamy skin and soft curves before she stopped his fingers.

"I want you," he whispered, reaching for her again. "Right here."

"I know," she whispered back, sitting on him and taking over the buttons herself. Slowly, smiling at him, she started to spread the material of her dress away. "But I'm in charge. You just have to lie there and enjoy. Do you like this?" A little more skin became exposed.

He nearly swallowed his tongue. "Yeah." Several more buttons opened and his pulse leaped in anticipation of her flesh against his.

"Are you sure?" she asked in a teasing tone. "Because I'm not quite positive you do."

"If I were any more sure," he said in a needy voice, "you'd be disappointed."

"Why?"

"It'd be over before you ever got my pants off."

She smiled a bit wickedly. "Then we'd just have to start again." Another button came undone, exposing another inch of flesh.

"You're enjoying this control thing, aren't you?"

"Mmm-hmm." Her fingers paused. Her dress parted slightly to her hips, revealing just enough pale blue lace to make his mouth go dry.

But a thread of doubt intruded into Clarissa's mind at the mix of shock and lust in his eyes, and she stopped. "It's okay with you that I'm enjoying this, isn't it?"

"Are you kidding?" His eyes never left her fingers as he struggled to sit up. "Don't you dare quit now."

She finished with the buttons, bit back the last of her insecurity, and spread her dress wide. The way his mouth dropped open a little, the way his body tensed, his fingers curling into the mat at his sides, all told her she was doing okay. More than okay, she realized when his gaze lifted to hers, hot and hungry.

"Come here, Clarissa."

God, that voice, she thought. So deep and sexy. She laughed a little, the joy and love in her heart releasing the terrible tension that had gripped her the past few days. "Stop talking," she told him. "I'm in charge here." Running her fingers down his bare chest, she teased and twirled the drawstring of his sweat bottoms. "I'm the seducer, remember?"

Steel clanged against steel as he shifted. "Well, Ms. Seducer, you have about two seconds to help me get out my leg braces or—" His words broke off as she slipped her hands boldly down his sweats to find him unbelievably hard and hot and ready.

He reached past her, struggling with the cuffs

and leather straps that had him so confined. As his hands raced blindly his mouth sought its own purchase, and latched onto a lace-covered breast. "Help me," he murmured as his tongue dipped past the barrier and found a pebbled nipple begging for his touch.

"Yes." Her hands fumbled with his. They were both swearing, sweating, and dying in less than a minute. One brace finally came loose, and Bo chucked it across the room. The other followed the same path, then his sweat bottoms and her bra.

"Now this," he vowed, slipping his thumbs into the lace at her hips and tugging off the wispy excuse for panties. Then he was pulling her down to straddle him, down to meet her hungry lips with his.

Holding her head with his kiss, he let his hands roam down her neck, over her aching breasts, and farther. With every caress the fire inside burned hotter and she whispered his name imploringly when his fingers found the spot between her legs that was already wet. In the next breath, his hands had gripped the backs of her thighs, spreading her legs wide and lifting her up over him.

"Bo—"

"It goes both ways," he growled into her mouth. "You master me and I master you. With passion, Clarissa. Never shame or anger, but this." And then he was inside her, and she struggled to catch her breath, but she relinquished her control without a care.

He filled her to the hilt. Bo's eyes closed and the back of his head hit the mat as he let out a soft groan. Fingers gripping her hips, he lifted her up, then let her sink slowly down, only to lift her up again.

Poised on the edge, Clarissa could only hold on and gasp for breath.

"Tell me now," he demanded, opening his dark eyes, eyes that shimmered with love and heat, while his damp chest heaved with the efforts of his breathing. "Tell me now when I'm deep inside you and you can hardly put a thought together." Even as he spoke, his fingers were on her, sure and slow, bringing her to an instant explosive climax.

Never had she been more thrilled to let go, to trust another person with her every movement, her every thought.

"Tell me," he repeated on a low, sandy breath as her eyes fluttered and struggled to stay open on him, her body still tremoring and quaking.

"I . . . love you." She gasped when he thrust up into her again. "I love you, Bo."

"I love you," he rasped, his fingers soothing even as he held her up over him. "God, how I love you."

With a choked cry, she shattered a second

time. She was still quivering when he came an instant later.

Neither of them moved, but shared a long, satisfied sigh. And as Bo's arms surrounded her Clarissa knew . . . she was home. She was safe. She was *loved*.

SIXTEEN

Bo grinned at Clarissa from flat on his back as she searched the gym floor in vain for her panties. "Go without," he suggested.

Stopping in the act of securing her bra, she gaped at him. "I can't go without my underwear!" she exclaimed so indignantly, he had to laugh.

He tripped her up so that she landed softly, right on him. As he ran a hand up the back of her thighs, his eyes darkened.

Her breath quickened. "*Can* I go without?" Her voice turned curious, almost hopeful, making him laugh again.

"You can do whatever you want." His heart kicked up three gears. With not nearly the grace he would have liked, he sat up and awkwardly straightened his legs, tucking Clarissa against his side when she would have risen. "As long as what you want is to marry me and spend the rest of your life seducing me during my nightly work-outs."

"Oh, Bo."

"And say my name like that, in exactly that breathless, sexy voice every time you look at me."

A teary smile crossed her face as she cupped his and kissed him. "You're my life," she said simply.

"Does that mean yes?"

"I thought you didn't want to get married."

"I didn't." Lifting her hand, he brushed the knuckles with a tender kiss before bringing it to his chest. Beneath their coiled fingers he could feel his heart drumming. "Until you."

Some of the joy drained from her face, and she tugged her hand free. "But you'll want children, and I'm not sure I can have them."

"If you can't, if *we* can't, then we won't. It doesn't matter to me, Clarissa. It's *you* I want. It's *you* I can't do without."

"But . . ." She let out a slow breath. "But I'm just a small-town girl, nothing like the women you're used to. Unsophisticated and drab. And I have a horrible accent!"

"I love unsophisticated and you could never be drab, not with that willowy, delicious body."

She blushed and bit her lip.

"And your incredibly sexy twang makes me hard."

"Bo!"

He laughed.

She crossed her arms over her chest. "You're not taking me seriously at all. I'm trying to save you a lot of trouble. What if I bore you?"

He laughed again, he couldn't help it. "Sweetheart, the woman who just seduced me on that mat will never bore me."

"It's more than sex."

"No kidding." But he dropped the teasing tone as he cupped her jaw. "It's about how you make me feel, how my heart warms whenever I see you. You make me laugh and hope and dream. You look at me and I feel such love—it's unbelievable how much. I can't do without that. There's nothing I want in this world more than you."

She stared at him, realizing she felt the same. Yes, he was devastatingly male. *Thank God.* She looked into his tanned handsome face, into melting brown eyes that promised today and a million tomorrows. Her future had never seemed so bright.

"God, Clarissa. Say something already. Say yes."

Skimming her fingers over his jaw to touch his cheek, she wondered . . . how could she have ever considered turning away from this man of her heart? She smiled. "Yes," she whispered as both laughter and tears escaped. "Yes, I want to marry you."

Eyes shining, Bo snatched her close. "Yes!" he whispered triumphantly, squeezing her tight.

But something had just occurred to Clarissa,

something awful. "Bo, what about your family? Won't they resent me for popping into your life so fast and stealing you?"

That caused him to laugh until tears fell. "Oh, Clarissa. Let me tell you about my family. . . ."

EPILOGUE

Four weeks later, and one day before Bo's birthday, Clarissa stood in his bathroom and stared down at the little stick in shock.

She had a million things to be doing, not the least of which was worrying about what to buy Bo for his birthday. What to buy the man who claimed he had everything he could ever want?

But though he was the most important thing in her life, Clarissa couldn't concentrate on that right now. Not when she was watching the stick as it slowly turned blue.

So did Clarissa.

Realizing she was holding her breath, she drew in air and promptly got dizzy. She sat, hard, right on the tile floor and stared at the stick some more.

Yep. It was blue.

"Oh, my God," she whispered, lifting an icy

hand to touch her flat belly. Nothing, she felt absolutely nothing.

Wait.

There. There it was. Deep inside, a warm, fuzzy feeling bubbled. A maternal, protective sort of feeling. A wonderful, huggy-kissy emotion she knew would never go away. Love washed over her.

She was pregnant and, after three short seconds of knowing, already madly in love with her child-to-be.

"Clarissa?" Bo knocked on the bathroom door. "You okay, sweetheart? We need to get going or we'll be late for work. And you know how Sheila gets a kick out of us being late."

"Come on in," she tried to say, but she had to clear her voice. She smiled through her sudden happy tears. "Oh, Bo. Hurry. I've got an early birthday present for you. . . ."

THE EDITOR'S CORNER

It is with much regret and a heartfelt sadness that I offer you a glimpse of next month's LOVESWEPTs, the last treats we will be able to present to you for the holidays. The December books will be the final romances published in the LOVESWEPT line. Savor these special holiday gifts from four of your favorite authors. Like every book we've published, they are truly keepers.

In the final chapter of the Mac's Angels series, Sandra Chastain brings you what you've been waiting for. LOVESWEPT #914, **THE LAST DANCE**, is Mac's very own love story. What would it take to get Mac to leave his secret mountain compound, Shangri-la, where he runs Angels Central? A chance to meet Sterling Lindsey turns out to be too much of a temptation for him to resist. Working for Mac's friend, Sterling has had enough contact with the mysterious head of the network of angels to know there's something special about him, something that draws her to him. On the way to their meeting she finds herself in mortal danger, and her faith in Mac is put to the test. Forced into hiding, they confront emotions they'd never dared confess. In this story of risk and romance, Sandra sends a lonely hero into the greatest battle of his life: to save the woman who'd kept his hope alive. Don't miss the outcome when the man who's played angel for everyone else finds his own bit of heaven.

Mary Kay McComas knows that simple pleasures are the best life has to offer, and she reinforces that idea in **BY THE BOOK**, LOVESWEPT #915. Ellen Webster is a self-described nice person. It's when she decides she's too nice for her own good that things begin to go awry. With assistance from a little self-help book, she sets out to reach for the stars, to go for the gusto in life . . . and Jonah Blake represents gusto with a capital G. The man everyone in town has been talking about has been watching Ellen with avid interest. While Jonah is minding the town's camera store for his ailing father, he can't keep his attention away from the beautiful redhead in the bank across the street. When Ellen and Jonah finally meet, it seems as if they're playing right into destiny's hands. But Ellen begins to worry that he's falling for the wrong woman—the New Ellen. In this wonderfully touching romance, Mary Kay teaches us once again that it isn't always necessary to reach for the stars when everything you could ever want is right here on earth.

No author captures the flavor of the South better than Charlotte Hughes, and **THE LAST SOUTHERN BELLE**, LOVESWEPT #916, is quintessential Charlotte. Heroine Annie Bridges had all the advantages growing up, but her father controlled her every move. When he handpicks a husband for her, Annie decides to show her rebellious side . . . and she chooses a fine time to do it—on her wedding day! She steals her father's limo and races off in her gown, not realizing until she's fifty miles out of town that she hasn't a dime to her name. Enter the hero, Sam Ballard, an attorney/business owner who is talked into giving Annie a job as a waitress at his diner. Annie is the worst waitress he's ever employed—and the most attractive. But after working closely with her, Sam discovers she has hidden talents for accounting and sales . . . and a few of a more intimate nature. Annie can't envision life with a confirmed bachelor such as Sam, but life without him is a bleaker prospect. As they begin to fall for each other, the past catches up with Annie, and she faces the toughest choice of all. Charlotte is sure to make you laugh through your tears with this, her final LOVESWEPT.

It is fitting and appropriate that we end LOVE-SWEPT with a romance by Fayrene Preston. Fayrene was among the six authors whose books were featured in our first month of publication, way back in May 1983. She has touched the hearts and minds of so many thankful readers that there was no question who would write the very last LOVESWEPT. And what a book it is! Ending her Damaron Mark series, Fayrene treats you to **THE PRIZE**, LOVESWEPT #917. With his cousins Sin and Lion happily paired off, Nathan is the last eligible Damaron. In Paris on business, he goes for a walk and is startled beyond belief when a beautiful woman runs up to him, throws her arms around him, and says, "Would you mind kissing me as if you're madly in love with me and are never going to let me go?" Of course, he complies with her request, but when she runs off with only a thank-you, Nathan is mystified . . . and intrigued. Before he can search for her, she shows up again, this time with an apology and an explanation. When Danielle Savourat discovers the man she kissed as part of a game is a Damaron, she realizes she must clear the air. What she doesn't realize is that Nathan has no intention of letting her get away this time. Fayrene sets a steamy course for these lovers as they learn what can happen with just one kiss.

With thanks and gratitude for your loyalty to LOVESWEPT,
All best wishes,

Susann Brailey

Susann Brailey

Senior Editor